YA Riorda
Riordan, James, 1936-
The sniper /

DISCARD

34028076191676
LAP $8.95   ocn243822025
11/01/10

3 4028 07619 1676
HARRIS COUNTY PUBLIC LIBRARY

LAP

THE
SNIPER

D0980703

For Yelena Alexandrovna

The Sniper copyright © Frances Lincoln Limited 2008
Text copyright © James Riordan 2008

First published in Great Britain in 2008 and in the USA in 2009
by Frances Lincoln Children's Books, 4 Torriano Mews,
Torriano Avenue, London NW5 2RZ

www.franceslincoln.com

All rights reserved.
No part of this publication may be reproduced, stored in a retrieval system,
or transmitted, in any form, or by any means, electrical, mechanical,
photocopying, recording or otherwise without the prior written permission
of the publisher or a licence permitting restricted copying. In the United Kingdom
such licences are issued by the Copyright Licensing Agency, Saffron House,
6-10 Kirby Street, London EC1N 8TS

A catalogue record for this book is available from the British Library.

ISBN: 978-1-84507-885-0

Printed in Croydon, Surrey, UK by CPI Bookmarque Ltd.
in December 2009

3 5 7 9 8 6 4 2

THE
SNIPER

JAMES RIORDAN

F
FRANCES LINCOLN
CHILDREN'S BOOKS

Everything in the world is beautiful, everything but our own thoughts and actions when we lose sight of the higher aims of life and our dignity as human beings.

Anton Chekhov

ONE

Night and day those eagle eyes search the city. They watch the deserted street below; they sweep tenement doorways and windows; they stare grimly at the smoking, silent buildings all around.

They look at the distant hills scarred with black craters. They hover over the steep slopes of Mamayev Kurgan, where only weeks ago children played in and out of the pine trees, families picnicked and lovers strolled hand in hand.

The once-green hill now runs red with blood. The wooded mound is now the iron mound, its slopes strewn with bullets and cartridge cases, mines and mortars, rusting gun batteries, charred hulks of tanks – some starred red, some crossed black.

The eyes narrow to a slit as they light upon the broad river. At night its inky waters are lit by exploding rockets, like cascading fireworks. By day they're silky-green like mermaid's hair, or scarlet-red as if the blood of war has flowed into them.

Night and day the city burns beneath a crimson sky – swirling with dust, shifting, rumbling, heavy and troubled.

The soldier's nose wrinkles at the acrid smoke that clogs the nostrils and scorches their tiny hairs. If only it could block out the suffocating stench of burning flesh.

Night and day the soldier's ears grow used to the fox-bark of gun and mortar fire, the lion-roar of tank and plane engines, the wolf-howl of rockets and shells – noises now as common as once were the rattling of trams, the deep-throated hoot of steamships, the merry chatter of children on their way to school.

Other sounds struggle to be heard. Red-nosed Stukas screech like owls diving on their prey. Screams – terrible, heart-rending, well up from the smoking rubble.

For a moment, in the deadly silence, music wafts through the air. Wet with dew drying in the sun, the telegraph wires catch the passing wind and together they sound like a violin that squeaks and hisses and trembles on the breeze.

Sometimes it is so quiet that the soldier can pick up the slightest sound from houses opposite: flakes of plaster falling pitter-patter like raindrops, the creak of jackboots and the rasp of German voices.

For days those eagle eyes have been seeking a nest. A broken bedroom window on the third floor? A gaping hole where once a bath stood? A door hanging from its hinge?

Finally, the sniper climbs to the top of the five-storey tenement. Here and there, steps and iron rails are missing and jagged holes yawn on the landings.

Those sharp eyes take in the contents of hastily-abandoned flats – a nickel-framed bedstead, a blackened bicycle, glittering shards of a shattered mirror, scorched tendrils of a palm tree on a window sill – the flesh and bones of a dead city. Each floor differs only in its faded paintwork: patchy-pink on the first floor, dark blue on the second, brown panels in pale violet on the third, pea-green, marigold…

The top landing gives a wide view of the city. Across and to the right stretch rows of gaunt apartment blocks. To the left lies a broad, arrow-straight boulevard leading to a square. All this is in German hands.

The landing is in the roof's shadow – hiding the sniper's rifle.

Night comes, turning the surrounding tenements into ogres brooding in the gloom. A full moon sails out from behind a purple bank of cloud and hangs in the night sky.

All at once a shadow flits across the window – a large smoky-grey cat with long fluffy tail passes by soundlessly, staring at the soldier through eyes lit by an electric-blue flame.

Somewhere down the road a dog barks, then a second and a third. An angry voice rings out, followed by a pistol shot and whimpering. Then again, a chorus of howls and baying begins. Dogs loyal to their home territory stop the enemy from moving around in the dark.

The sniper peers about. Swift, dark figures loom in the shadows, carrying sacks and pillows into the block opposite. A shot would give the game away.

Carefully, to avoid treading on broken glass glinting in the moonlight, the sniper stands up and climbs cautiously down to the basement.

The basement is home to an infantry unit – or what's left of it. The duty sergeant lies snoring on an iron bedstead. His men are lying on singed strips of velvet curtains and thick woollen blankets.

Someone winds up the gramophone, calling out, 'What's it to be, lads?'

Voices chorus back, 'Same as ever.' There's only one unbroken record.

A solemn baritone starts to sing:

'A blizzard rages beyond the window…'

The soldiers sit quietly until the singer reaches the chorus. Then they all join in:

'Milady Death, we beg you:
Wait a while outside the door.'

Sitting on a pile of books in a dark corner of the cellar, the sniper senses the sadness in the song. So does the sergeant, now wide awake. He wipes away a tear and sits up, making the bedsprings creak and groan.

'Hey, sniper, how many Fritzes have you done for today?'

The sniper ignores him, thoughts elsewhere, then glances up and murmurs to the soldiers, 'Don't play that music tomorrow.'

***

Next morning the sniper is up before sunrise with a flask of water and some biscuits, stretched out on the cold stone floor, rifle resting on the steel window-frame. And waits...

So strong is the morning sun that even the charred city manages a wan smile. Only beneath the roof where the sniper lies is there a cold grey shadow.

All of a sudden, every sinew in the sniper's body tenses.

Round the corner of the block opposite appears a German; he is carrying an enamel bucket. Precisely at this time, the morning soldier fetches water for the officer's early wash.

The sniper flicks the range-finder's fly-wheel until the thin black cross meets a spot four centimetres from the tip of the soldier's nose – then unhurriedly squeezes the trigger. The head jerks back and something dark spurts from under the grey-green cap; the pail falls with a clatter and the man topples sideways.

'One.'

A moment later, a second German turns the corner. He's carrying a pair of black binoculars.

The sniper fires again.

'Two.'

A third man appears, bent low, running towards the fallen soldiers.

'Three.'

At this point the sniper makes a mental note: better to fire at a running than a standing figure.

The sniper's eyes see so much. They spot the path that runners take to staff headquarters, scraps of paper in their hands.

They note the track down which they go to fetch bread and water for drinking and washing.

They notice the road along which they bring grenades and ammunition to feed the mortars and machine-guns.

The Germans eat their food cold. The sniper knows their lunch and supper menu: black bread, coffee and tinned meat. Before each meal they always open up a mortar barrage, as regular as clockwork: it lasts half an hour, not a minute more or less. Then there is silence, followed by a shout: 'Hey, Russky, time to eat!'

This drives the sniper mad. How dare they play games in this miserable, dead city, offending every sense of decency! The sniper is especially merciless at meal-times.

Towards the end of the day, the sniper catches sight of a German officer. He's walking tall and arrogant – a Big Noise, strutting about in his long leather coat, shiny peaked cap and black gloves. Soldiers come rushing out of dooways, standing to attention and saluting.

Once more the sniper calmly adjusts the rifle sights and takes careful aim. The arm holding the rifle tingles with pins and needles, but the hand is as steady as a rock, and prepares to fire against the background of a white wall – so that the flash and puff of smoke can't be seen against the glare of the sunlit wall.

A single shot rings out.

The officer shakes his head as if stung. He throws up

his hands and falls backwards into the dirt, his shiny boots pointing towards the hidden assassin.

'Four.'

The sniper has an overwhelming urge to stop Germans strutting about the city, to make them cower and cringe. By the end of the day they no longer walk upright. They scurry about like frightened rats, their bodies half-bent, keeping to the shadows.

By the end of the second day, they are beginning to crawl. The track they used to fetch water is now deserted. No longer do officers take an early morning wash. No longer do the men have fresh water; they have to make do with stale water from the boilers.

Towards evening of the second day, pressing the trigger, the sniper smiles grimly.

'Seventeen sticks.'

The sniper always calls Germans 'sticks' – to be snapped in two, broken, smashed, stamped on. They're not human beings. This makes killing easier.

That night the Germans go without their supper. No longer do they shout, 'Russky, time to eat!' Nor do they venture out for shells and ammunition.

All night long there is the clang of picks and shovels as the sappers dig tunnels in the hard soil.

'Good, I've driven you into the ground,' says the sniper, and goes downstairs to sleep.

TWO

War came without warning. In the night. Under cover of darkness.

Like snakes in the grass, the Germans slithered across the border and pounced on their unwary prey. At dawn in every town and village, loudspeakers crackled and coughed out the grim news.

Even before the echoes of death had died away, Hitler's armies were blitzing their way through the rough and ready defences. Brest fell, Minsk. Kiev. Kharkov. Not far now to Stalingrad. And once past 'the City-on-the-Volga', the way would be clear to Moscow.

Stalingrad awaited its fate. The heavens shook to the tramp of German jackboots, the crunch of tank treads, the drone of Heinkels and Messerschmitts. But for the moment the earth was still, the feather grass swayed in the summer breeze, the river rippled to gusts of wind. How long? How long? A month... a week... days? How soon would it be before the streets were battlefields, each house a fortress, underground sewers the only escape route? How soon before the waters turned red with blood?

For the moment, the people of Stalingrad carried on as normal: the children went to school, played hopscotch and football in the sun-baked yard. Tania's mother tended sick children in the nearby hospital. Her father fed the furnaces in the Red October Steel Works. And Tania's younger brothers, Vadim and Misha, accompanied her to school each day chattering merrily, without a care in the world.

One morning, an announcement was made to the senior classes:

'Boys and girls. The Head wants you all lined up in the yard.'

'Oh no!' groaned Boris behind Tania, 'Not collecting more scrap metal. There can't be a single tin can left in the whole of Russia.'

Tania and her classmates formed three rows in the playground.

The Head didn't keep them waiting long in the hot sun. A tall, unsmiling man, he had served in three wars and lost something in each: an eye in World War I, his left arm in the Revolution, and his right leg in the Civil War. Now he limped on to a makeshift platform of old melon boxes to address them.

'Young people,' he began hoarsely. As if uncertain how to continue, he squinted sternly with his good eye at each face before him.

'Dig for Victory!' he finally managed.

The children looked puzzled. Dig? What with?

His deputy stepped into the breech. A middle-aged woman, she was as round as she was tall – 'Miss Square Metre', they called her.

'Attention! Your mission is to sandbag the city petrol

tanks. Got it? P-e-t-r-o-l T-a-n-k-s.'

Was that all?

The mass sigh of disappointment visibly displeased Miss Square Metre. She was used to being instantly obeyed, no questions asked. But with the Head's good eye on her, she broke her own rule, and went on:

'Petrol is inflammable. What does "inflammable" mean?'

Without waiting for an answer, she said, 'Right, it burns easily. You all know that. So if the Germans drop a fire-bomb near the petrol dump, the whole lot will go up in flames. Got it?'

Then, with a sigh, she added, 'Petrol is the city's life-blood. How do we protect our life-blood? By filling sacks with sand... and lagging the storage tanks.'

The beetle-browed, blue-jawed Head broke in: 'This is urgent! A race against time... Senior Pioneers, take charge!'

THREE

Tania shifted uneasily as chins wagged and eyebrows rose about her. This wasn't part of her plans. She'd set her heart on becoming a children's doctor, like her mother, or maybe a dancer. Since she was small and skinny, she danced in a ballet group – someone had said she might one day dance with the Bolshoi in Moscow. Doctor? Yes. Ballerina? Maybe. Sandbag filler – definitely not!

Meanwhile, an old bushy-bearded man in ragged brown overalls had arrived to lead the way. He introduced himself as Uncle Fedya.

'Now, kiddies, off we go.'

'Where to, Uncle Fedya?' asked one of the boys gruffly, offended at being called 'kiddies'.

'Where to?' the old man mumbled. 'The graveyard, of course.'

The children followed him two abreast, wondering what graveyards had to do with petrol tanks.

'Maybe we have to dig up dead bodies and put them in sacks instead of sand,' said Boris, to scare the girls.

'Don't be daft,' Tania's friend Nina said. 'The sacks wouldn't be big enough.'

'We'll have to chop them up,' said Boris, 'or maybe just stack them round the tanks.'

Lena interrupted.

'Shut up, Boris. If you saw a dead body, you'd dive into the river.'

Uncle Fedya led them to a tumbledown shed in the nearby graveyard, unlocked the door and poked about inside. The schoolchildren glanced about fearfully at the graves – some with crooked crosses, some with red stars, many with faded photos of smiling faces. After a few minutes he reappeared.

'Here, lads, grab hold of these!' he yelled. He handed out six spades, two shovels, a wheelbarrow and eight planks of wood.

'That's all the tools we've got. Do your best. Off you go. And make sure you bring them back.'

With the wheelbarrow in front, the troupe marched off, shovels and spades over their shoulders, planks under their arms – for all the world like Snow White's seven dwarfs. But they weren't heading for a diamond mine.

The petrol dump was a tidy walk away, sitting on a cliff like a black-and-white-striped lighthouse. It overlooked the river on one side, and the dusty steppe on the other.

The senior Pioneer, Rosa, divided up the forty young people into teams of five, giving each a spade or shovel or plank of wood. Boris took charge of the wheelbarrow.

'Don't forget what the Head said,' cried Rosa. 'This is urgent. So get cracking!'

Rosa smiled to hear herself talking like this. Who was she kidding? What was the hurry? There was no sign of Germans: on land, on river or in the sky. The authorities were always frightening people – to make them work harder, fulfil the plan, uncover 'enemies of the people'. And now she was scaring them, telling them the Germans were coming...

It was tough in the baking midday heat. No rain had fallen for a couple of months and the temperature was now well into the forties. When the wind blew off the steppe it was hot, dry and dusty, making you lick your lips and take in gulps of river breeze.

The teams were soon soaked in sweat with only cotton headscarves to protect their heads from the merciless sun. They dug, heaped wooden planks with sandy soil, and stumbled over the rough earth with their loads.

Tania and her best friend Maya carried a plank piled with sand to and fro, from trench to wall, wall to trench. Their feet were soon cut and bleeding from the hard-baked earth, backs and arms aching from the strain, breath coming in short gasps as they sucked in the stifling air.

They did their best to treat it as a game: boys against girls, fifteens versus sixteens, one team against another. Now and then, Rosa urged them on from the top of a mound.

'Well done, Pioneers! Heroes of Labour! Your Motherland needs you!'

Wiping the sweat from her eyes, Tania grinned at the grunts and the eager, dirt-streaked faces of her friends. She felt a thrill at being part of this new game...

Until...

FOUR

From out of nowhere, a swarm of mosquitoes appeared in the cloudless blue sky. No, not mosquitoes, they were wasps. No, not wasps... black crows. No, not crows... huge vultures.

The children stood like statues, staring. It was too late to dive for cover. They'd never seen a German plane before.

'Are they ours or theirs?' someone cried.

'If they're ours,' Boris laughed, 'we'd better take cover!'

A plane suddenly peeled off and dived towards the youngsters, its guns spitting bullets, real bullets. The earth around them spurted little fountains of dirt, like hail-stones in the sand.

'Dive for cover!' yelled Lena. 'Before they come back!'

The trenches they'd been digging now found a use – as shelters.

But the fighter plane that had dropped iron rain did not return. Instead, another, stubbier aircraft dropped a bomb on the cliff, destroying the children's good work in seconds. It thudded into the soft earth, sending up a shower of clods and clumps and sand that seemed to hang in the air before tumbling back down to earth. A blanket of flying soil smothered them all.

For a moment, Tania's face was squashed into the sand. She couldn't breathe. She couldn't see. She could hear a dull drone, a heavy weight was pressing on her back, pushing her down. Frantically she wriggled and squirmed, pushing herself up, fighting for dear life. She spat out soil, coughing furiously to clear her lungs.

Once she could see clearly, her first thought was: 'Is anybody hurt?' No. Apart from bumps and bruises, everyone seemed to have escaped unharmed.

Then all at once a cry went up:

'Where's Rosa? Where's Nina?'

Now the digging had a more urgent purpose: to find the girls before they choked to death. But where were they?

With their bare hands the children frantically scraped and scooped, clearing away the dirt, not daring to use wooden shovels or pointed sticks. Tania winced as sharp stones cut into her hands.

After what seemed an age, a desperate cry rang out: 'Over here! Quick! I think it's Rosa.'

Almost at once, another half-strangled yell: 'Here!'

It was Nina.

The children's dusty, sweaty faces grinned with relief. But not for long.

They quickly pulled out Rosa, with nothing more than a few cuts and shock. But Nina was obviously in a bad way.

'Uhhh... uhhh...' she whimpered, when her mouth

was wiped clean. 'My back! My back!'

The children stood round her helplessly. What should they do?

If ever there was a moment for testing Tania's first aid skills, this was it. She took charge like a seasoned nurse, imitating her mother's confident tones, though inside she was shaking.

'Don't move her! Clear away the soil. Give her air.'

Turning round, she shouted to two boys, 'Vitya, Sasha! Wheelbarrow. Make it snappy!'

All the while, she was brushing crumbs of earth from Nina's mouth, nose and eyes, murmuring words of comfort.

'Keep still, Ninochka. We'll get you out. Don't worry, little pigeon. You'll be fine, just fine.'

'I can't f-f-feel my l-l-legs,' Nina spluttered, spitting earth, her wild eyes showing panic.

Tania was swiftly going over the possibilities: no sign of blood. The injuries must be internal. But what were they? Nina couldn't move. Paralysed temporarily from shock? Hopefully. Or... from a broken back? If so, they must be careful moving her. A wheelbarrow wouldn't be any use.

'Boys,' she shouted, 'put some planks across the barrow.'

Vitya and Sasha were standing beside the wheelbarrow. Now, under Tania's guidance... ever so slowly... several pairs of hands eased Nina out and on to the planks.

Tania gave one last order.

'Someone run back to school. Tell them what's happened. One thing's for sure: the Germans will be back.'

FIVE

No one questioned Tania's command. She astonished herself. Was this really her? Little Tania Belova, bossing boys and girls older than her? The mere thought made her shrink back into her shell. She was a follower, not a leader. But they had to get Nina to hospital double quick; she looked ghastly.

Tania led the way to hospital. Poor Nina groaned and grimaced with pain as Sasha and Vitya trundled the wheelbarrow over the cobblestones of Komsomol Prospect. Shabby trams clattered by, frightened white faces staring out of their dusty windows. Carts carrying shells for anti-aircraft guns rattled cheerfully in the opposite direction. They passed the old market with stalls weighed down under great piles of tomatoes and cucumbers, jars of yellow sunflower oil and huge bottles of amber-coloured baked milk.

Despite the air raid, old women in padded grey jackets and long brown headscarves were still shouting, 'Cucumbers. Tomatoes. Honey.'

It was odd, life going on as if nothing had happened.

The children had just turned a corner when they stopped in their tracks. A dead soldier was lying on his back, arms outstretched, a cigarette end stuck to his lips. A still-smoking stub. Just a moment before there'd been life, thoughts, dreams. Now, in a flash, death.

They had never seen a dead body before. It looked no different from someone sleeping. No blood. No arms or legs broken off. No bullet holes in the jacket. He looked so peaceful, a wispy fair moustache curling up in a surprised half-smile. At any moment Tania expected him to open his eyes and wink at them. Yet he was stone dead. No doubt about it.

The three of them hurried on with Nina. All at once they found themselves in Central Square. A shot-down plane – a Heinkel, someone said – lay sprawled across the asphalt, with neat black crosses and a lion on a shield, for all the world as if it was on a Crusade. There was no sign of the pilot.

'Good! We've made them pay for hurting Nina,' Tania said aloud with a scowl. 'That pilot deserved to die, the coward – attacking without warning.'

Children were crawling over the plane's broken wings, squeezing into the cockpit and fiddling with the instruments. Men in suits stood staring at the wreck, women with bright lipstick were gaping at the metal bird that had buried its talons into the earth.

'Come on, lads,' Tania urged the two boys. 'Not far now.'

Nina was drifting in and out of sleep, her eyes shut tight. When they reached the hospital, they pushed the wheelbarrow into Reception and, after giving details to a duty nurse, they were swiftly shooed out. No thanks. No questions. No time. But as they went, Nina suddenly opened her eyes wide and looked up. She blinked three times – by way of thanks to each of them. Tears came to Tania's eyes as she squeezed Nina's hand. She wouldn't die, would she?

Once outside, they felt lost: too shaken to go home, too tired to rejoin their school-mates, too excited to do nothing.

'There's no point in going back,' said Sasha. 'Better see the damage.'

'Why don't we climb Mamayev Kurgan?' suggested Vitya. 'You can see the whole of Stalingrad from the top.'

They needed to empty their lungs, breathe in fresh air and distance themselves from the shock of the bombing. Silently, the three of them walked towards the hill above the river. After much huffing and puffing they reached the top, collapsed on to the bare ground and gazed about.

The view was breathtaking. Not only could they look across the city to the west, they could see far beyond the river to the vast meadowlands in the east, with their tiny islands of white huts.

The sprawling city clung to the high bank for miles and miles, like a giant caterpillar, as far as the eye could see. New stone buildings stood out like islands in an ocean of wooden shacks. Clusters of tumbledown, windowless huts straggled along the edge of ravines, crept down to the riverside and clambered up the cliffs, squeezing themselves between tall, concrete tenements.

On the northern horizon stood the vast Tractor Plant,

now making tanks and lorries. Other great smoking factories – the Lazur Chemical Plant, Barricades and Red October – were belching sooty clouds from tall chimneys, accompanied by the clanking of cranes and the whistling of trains.

Red October was where Dad worked in the foundry. He'd helped build the plant from scratch, brick by brick. He was very proud, holding up of his calloused hands and boasting, 'That's Red October hands for you!' How long would the factory remain standing now? Tania wondered.

Past everything flowed the River Volga, broad and unruffled, separating the grime and bustle of one bank from the vast virgin plain beyond.

The shimmering river was full of pine-log rafts, caravans of barges, ferry boats, tugs and fussy, smoke-begrimed launches, all hooting and whistling at each other in their riverboat tongue. They were trailing wreaths of smoke and oil which intermingled like paint running on an artist's canvas. An ancient steamer, its paddles thrashing the water, puffed along leisurely against the current.

At first glance, the city and river looked as they always did on a sunny summer's day. But look closer, and here and there black smoke and red flames could be seen rising to the skies: blood was beginning to ooze from the city's wounds.

SIX

When Tania arrived back at her family's flat overlooking the river, she found everyone in a panic.

'Oh, thank God you're safe!' cried her mother, throwing her arms round her daughter and kissing her face and hair as if she'd been away for months.

'Mum, leave off, I'm fine,' Tania cried, pulling herself away. 'Not even a scratch.'

She told her story: the petrol tanks, the bomb, Nina hurt, the stretcher party, the crashed enemy plane, the awesome view from the hill.

Her twelve-year old brother, Misha, had his own news. He burst out, 'Daddy's gone to fight the Fascists!'

Mum and Tania looked at each other. Dad had received his call-up papers months ago. But he'd been kept back for war work. Now he could be spared. Women of all ages were feeding the furnaces, hammering molten metal, building tanks. They worked round the clock non-stop in fourteen-hour shifts, with no days off.

Proudly, Mum announced with a catch in her voice, 'Your Dad's been attached to General Rodimtsev's Rifle Division – defending Stalingrad.'

The children looked at her open-mouthed.

'We'll be safe now, with Dad to defend us,' declared Misha.

'No more school!' piped up eight-year-old Vanya.

'Maybe,' said Mum hesitantly. 'No school for a few weeks, anyway. Teachers will be busy chasing Hitlerites back to Berlin.'

She had a sudden thought.

'Talking of teachers, Tania, the school phoned. You're to report in the morning. Something about gunners.'

Tania was surprised.

'Gunners? I've never fired a gun in my life.'

'It's all hands to the pump now,' said Mum. 'That awful raid today won't be the last. We're at war now.'

'What's war?' asked Vanya.

'War? War's war,' said his mother slowly, wondering how to explain the horrors she remembered as a seven-year-old from twenty years earlier. 'War's bombing and shooting. Lots of people getting killed.'

'We'll win, won't we?' asked Misha anxiously.

'Yes!' said his mother firmly.

Then she added, 'It may take a little time. The Germans may have more planes and tanks, and they're keen to finish before winter. We may have to retreat a couple of steps... to advance three steps later.'

'But,' cried Vitya, 'Marshal Stalin said, "Not a step back!" I heard it on the wireless last month.'

Mother fell silent, a frown puckering her brow. Dad was always saying to her, 'Walls have ears.' And she didn't want to be heard going against the Leader. Someone might report her.

Tania said firmly, 'They may think they'll blow down

our door, but they're in for a shock. Remember the pig who built his house of bricks? Well, is our house made of bricks?'

Vanya banged his little fist against the wall.

'Ouch! Yep. It's brick.'

'There you are, then,' she exclaimed. 'We're as safe as houses.'

But in her heart, she wasn't sure. Nina. The dead soldier. Who would be next?

SEVEN

Next morning at 8.30 on the dot, Tania lined up in the school yard with everyone else. A nervous tingle ran through the ranks of fifteen and sixteen-year olds at the sight of a squad of soldiers standing to attention behind the Head.

The sun was blazing, adding to the stifling atmosphere. No one, not even Boris, was in a joking mood today – not after yesterday. This was serious. The Head soon made that clear.

Leaning heavily on a stick, he said sombrely, 'Young people. My children. Lads and lasses…'

He wasn't quite sure how to address his pupils. These children were to fight a war. Many would die. These could be the last days of their lives.

'Young Pioneers!' At last he'd struck the right note. 'Young Pioneers, yesterday you defended your homeland with valour. Not, of course, without cost. Our brave Nina Ulanova is in hospital. You must avenge her.'

His stern, one-eyed gaze passed over the young people before him.

'For you, your schooling is at an end,' he continued hoarsely. 'Good luck to you all. I entrust you to Captain Sarkisyan.' And a hush descended as the Head turned slowly and hobbled off. Although no one was very fond of him, he had their respect.

'Comrades!' barked a stocky officer in Red Army uniform. That got their attention. They weren't used to being called 'Comrades', and the word was spoken with a strong Armenian accent.

'Comrades, your country needs you. Your city, your home, your loved ones need you to defend them. Time is short. I call on volunteers.'

Volunteers? Volunteer for what?

A buzz of expectancy ran through the ranks. A few of the older boys led an army chant, 'Ooo-rah! Ooo-rah! Ooo-rah!'

'Good. Line up in two assignment groups, boys to the left, girls to the right!'

They shuffled about, uncertain whether he meant his left or their left. Finally, they sorted themselves out and waited for further orders.

Captain Sarkisyan and two soldiers walked up and down the rows, as if on a tour of inspection. It was a bit like picking sides for a football match. The officer selected the big and brawny, girls as well as boys, for mortar crews, and the slim and quick as scouts and runners.

Just a handful of girls and boys remained, as always happened in pick-up teams. Tania was one of them, and she wasn't pleased.

While the mortar crews and scouts were led away, the rejects stood waiting to be sent back to class or assigned to medical duties. But they were in for a shock.

'You lucky people!' cried the captain, with a crafty

wink to his men. 'You are the quick and the brave. *Ack-ack. Ack-ack. Ack-ack!'*

A startled girl put up her hand.

'Excuse me, Sir, what's *ack-ack?*'

He looked stunned.

'You'll find out, Comrade,' he snorted.

Soldiers marched them off in single file to a gun range on a deserted part of the river bank. It was all new and exciting. Each pupil was issued with army fatigues, much too big and baggy, floppy green helmets and brown army boots. Talk about a circus of clowns! thought Tania.

But Captain Sarkisyan soon wiped the smiles off their faces.

'You're in the army now! The Red Army. Anyone I catch with as much as a crooked grin will have his eyeballs pulled down his nose! Got it?'

'Got it!' they echoed back as one.

'Right, now to work.'

Over the next few days they did a crash course in firing guns. Not any old guns, but big, mounted, long-barrelled cannons which turned with a wheel. They worked in threes: one (Lena) to wind the handle, raising the guns to various elevations, one (Maya) to feed the gunner with long, shiny shells, and the gunner (Tania, since she was the smallest).

They aimed at pretend-enemy targets – a bluff of sandy cliff (Tania hoped there were no rabbits about).

At first Tania was scared stiff of the thunderous noise, of the stink of gun-smoke, of hitting her own people.

But once she'd got the hang of it, she lost her nervousness. She was more afraid of the army instructors, forever bullying and threatening. They made no allowance for tender young ears.

'Higher! Lower! Up! Down!'

'Son-of-a-bitch! Faster! Stop! Start!'

'Go! *Sukin syn!*'

'Come on! Fire! Fire! Fire!'

This was no game. Tania knew that. Today practice, tomorrow the real thing. She remembered the Heinkel on Central Square and dreamed of shooting down enemy planes. Revenge for Nina. An eye for an eye, a tooth for a tooth. She would have to postpone her nursing duties.

EIGHT

No one knew when the enemy would arrive. Already from the west giant columns of dust were rising up like whirlwinds. The clouds moved closer, ever closer, eastwards, across the grassy steppe. The spiralling towers of dust concealed soldiers of the German Sixth Army. In three long years of war, Hitler's Army had never suffered defeat. And now it was approaching the gates of Stalingrad.

The darkest hour comes just before the dawn... 4.30 a.m. on Sunday 23rd August, to be precise. This was the date and time Hitler had planned for taking the city. The Führer liked order.

Dawn came up to the thunder of tank engines, shattering the eerie silence of the steppe. Hundreds of Panzer tanks ('panthers') roared forward, turning the sky from grey to brilliant yellow, orange, violet, crimson and, finally, blood-red.

On the streets of the city, the loudspeakers spluttered to life.

'Attention. Attention. Citizens... this is an air raid warning! This is an air raid warning!'

People were puzzled. They'd had endless false alarms during the previous week. Like the boy who cried 'Wolf!' few people took alarms seriously any more.

For Tania, lying snugly next to her two brothers, the broadcast was as good as a military command. She tumbled out of bed, dressed in her fatigues in double-quick time, said goodbye to her mother and rushed helter-skelter to her sand-bagged battery. Within fifteen minutes she was sitting in front of her gun-barrels pointing up at the dark empty sky. Maya, the shell-feeder, stood ready; Lena, the gun-winder had raised the barrels.

This was it! The real thing! There was no fear, no trembling hands, no butterflies fluttering in tummies. Something inside took hold of Tania as she gazed at the shifting dark clouds and fading moon. An odd sense of calm gripped her, as if this was the most natural act in the world, like plaiting her blond pigtails.

'FIRE!' came the command.

Where? What at – a dove-grey canopy of sky with tiny squiggles of early-morning gulls? Where were the planes?

'FIRE!'

They let off a salvo.

'But we can't see anything,' complained Maya to the young commander.

'Then wipe the sleepy dust from your eyes!' he yelled.

Maya meekly wiped her eyes with the back of her hand, peered into the gloom… and still saw nothing.

'FIRE!'

Boom, boom, boom.

Small black puffs of smoke exploded in the grey-blue sky – hitting nothing but thin air.

An hour passed. And another. Tania's bloodshot eyes

kept closing for lack of sleep, her hands ached as she gripped the gun barrel, her mind kept seeing faces in the sky: snarling, leering one minute, smiling, beaming the next.

Early morning passers-by were shading their eyes, peering into the rising sun to try to spot something. The gun crews did likewise, each vying to be the first to shout a warning, like the look-out in a crow's-nest.

Then they saw them.

Hundreds of planes in the west, coming from the River Don. Row after row of migrating geese flying in V-formation – Stukas and Junkers, all droning towards the city. They'd never seen so many planes, never dreamed so many existed. The aircraft came on and on in an unending stream – so many, it was hard to know where they were heading. They were flying in neat groups, at different levels.

'How can we stop them all?' wondered Tania. 'Do we have enough shells and guns to prevent them getting through? If this is what we're up against...'

She didn't dare finish her thoughts.

NINE

'FIRE! FIRE! FIRE!'

It was impossible not to hit them. The whole sky was studded with exploding black and red stars. Yet no matter how many were hit, still they came on. On and on and on. They were flying so low, Tania could see their yellow wing-tips, white-edged black crosses and bulging undercarriages.

As she waited for Maya to reload and Lena to set the elevation, she watched the lead plane turn upside down, its red wheels in the air, tipping into a screaming dive. Little black spots began to fall like sooty rain.

One, two, three, four, five, six... ten... twelve... She counted them as she fired Maya's shells.

Right, you black-hearted Nazis, take that... and that. This one's for Nina! This one's for the dead soldier!

The noise was deafening, making her ears throb. The entire earth shook as from an earthquake. Everything was covered in a dense cloud of smoke and dust. No longer could she see where the guns were pointing. Yet still she fired back, aimlessly, hopelessly, hit-and-miss.

In a break in the smoke clouds she saw more bombs raining down, bundles of sticks that swirled lazily as they fell. Incendiaries showered down on wooden cottages. After the long drought, the flames spread like wildfire;

ash and débris were sucked up into the air as through a chimney.

Concussion bombs blew down most of the apartment blocks on Gogol and Pushkin avenues. The city waterworks suffered a direct hit; so did the railway station and the telephone exchange. No more water. No more trains. No more phone calls. Next to go were the petrol tanks that the Pioneer brigade had tried so hard to protect. A ball of fire and black smoke shot high into the sky, spewing flaming oil across the river.

Tania worked feverishly, burning her hands as she helped Lena and Maya throw out the spent shells, reloading, cranking the metal handle. Amidst the shriek of bombs and boom of guns, the searing heat and choking smoke, she had no notion of night and day.

Four days and nights without rest. Load, aim, fire. Load, aim, fire. Load, aim, fire…

Was it really blood that flowed through her veins? No sooner did her eyelids begin to close, than it seemed someone sprinkled water on them and she was wide-eyed and alert again. Load, aim, fire!

Got him!

She remembered lining up her sights and firing at a dark oblong box flying through the clear dawn skies. All at once, it shuddered as if caught in an invisible spider's web. Black smoke billowed out of the back as from a revving truck, and swirling soot clouds climbed upwards into fading shafts of moonlight. Then the stricken plane tipped over and nose-dived, down, down,

down… It reminded her of a falling sycamore seed, spiralling to the ground, round and round and round.

Her metal seat shook as the plane rammed the river-bank and burst into flames. It wasn't like a bonfire where logs sizzle and take fire stubbornly. These were exploding billows of white-hot and fiery-red flames, each expanding like ripples on a pond, then slowly fading to the steady burning of a well-lit fire.

If Tania felt sorry for the pilot trapped inside the inferno, she didn't show it, as she shared delight with her two gunner comrades.

'That'll teach them!' she cried.

She wanted to shoot down more and more. She was in a frenzy: shove in another shell, twist the handle. Aim, fire! Aim, fire! Aim, fire!

Though Tania didn't know it, she had shot down nine enemy planes. The last thing she remembered was feeling dizzy. It happened in a flash. Sweat mingled with something sticky on the back of her head as she clung desperately to the gun to stop herself falling. Someone grabbed her arm, and she glimpsed Maya's white face, with round blue eyes and open mouth from which no sound emerged.

Then everything vanished. The gun battery melted away and she found herself lying on something warm and soft that squirmed beneath her. She clutched at it, as a drowning person might a floating log. Whatever it was crawled away, and she sank down, down, down into a deep, dark pit…

TEN

Dimly, as in a speeded-up silent film, Tania felt herself being picked up by rough hands, bundled into an ambulance – or was it a wheelbarrow? – and bumping along rutted roads. Then came a sudden halt, the banging of doors, daylight, the marshy smell of the river, being carried up stone steps, through a padded doorway, then… dropped into a chocolate blancmange. The last thing she remembered was the broad back of a figure in a blood-stained smock disappearing through the door. Then she sank into the chocolate mousse, dead to the world.

***

She woke up stiff and racked with pain. As her eyes slowly grew accustomed to the light, she saw dust swirling all about her like river mist. For a brief moment she thought she was floating on a chocolate cloud in a chocolate paradise. But, no… She sniffed the air and smelled gunpowder. Grit was in her teeth, nose, eyes, down the back of her neck. As she unclenched her fists, her fingers touched something cold and solid: a leather sofa.

On the rug beside the dark brown sofa were broken plates, reddish pools, curly green leaves and a mash of bean, carrot and beetroot. Right in the centre of the parquet floor was a big, jagged chunk of concrete set in glittering fragments of glass. All the windows were broken.

Painfully, she hauled herself up and swung her legs to the floor. Her back ached as though someone had beaten it black and blue with a wooden club. And her hands! Raw flesh showed pink through blackened skin. They hurt like hell. On the crown of her head was a crusty lump stuck to her tangled hair; she felt it gingerly to see if her head was still stuck to her body.

It was. She had a head. She was alive.

She dragged herself to her feet and, as she took a few faltering steps, she could tell she was still in the land of the living by the pain that jolted her entire body. Halfway across she stopped. Suddenly it hit her.

'I'm home!' she muttered, startled at the croak of her own voice. 'But where is everyone?'

It must be four or five days since she'd left home. Her brothers had been fast asleep, as innocent as lambs. Dad had already left to join his unit. Now they had all vanished, as if whisked away by a whirlwind.

A terrible thought came to her. Oh, no...

Her heart beating fast, she knelt on the floor and dipped a finger into the dark red pool, putting it to her tongue. Salty. Earthy. Tasty. Definitely not blood.

She heaved a sigh of relief.

But where were they? Sheltering? Evacuated? Taken prisoner?

The realisation that she was alone sent chills up and down Tania's spine. In all her sixteen years she'd never been alone before, not knowing where her family was, when they'd return. Perhaps she would be alone for ever?

Angrily, she pushed away the scary thought. She hobbled out on to the balcony and gazed disbelievingly across the city.

The railway station was burning. The building beside it was also on fire. What was it? Oh, yes, the Secret Police Headquarters. Tania had always looked away whenever she passed, for fear of being dragged inside.

To the left, towards the grain elevator, everything was a-glow. The main square was empty of life. Craters scarred the grey asphalt. A body was lying spread-eagled beside the stone fountain. A rickety cart lay abandoned, the horse sitting on its hindquarters, unable to rise. Smoke covered the entire square.

South of the city Tania could hear the staccato beat of explosions like Chinese crackers. She guessed that an ammunition truck had been hit, setting off shells in batches.

On the street below were scores of people, some with big bundles, some with carts or prams. They were running, staggering, hurrying along as their belongings kept falling off. Glass crunched and popped like seaweed beneath their feet. Long, orange tongues of flame were leaping out of the tenement opposite, licking the walls of the corner house, climbing swiftly upwards, even as firemen nearby were unwinding their hoses.

The sun was setting, yet it was still light. Above the city the sky gleamed red – whether from fires or setting sun, who could tell? In the distance three lofty columns of smoke thrust their way up through the air, dense and black as soot lower down, grey and streaky as they rose higher – until they ran together into a single unbroken cloud.

Along the eastern riverbank, golden aspen and silver birch trees still stood – slender, graceful, delicate as lace.

Stalingrad was burning. Not just factories, but offices, buildings, homes – the entire western bank, as far as the eye could see. This was the way the tinder-dry forest burned – for weeks on end, over hundreds of square kilometres.

Black on red. Red on red. Black on black.

Black city.

Red sky.

The Volga, too, ran red, like blood.

ELEVEN

Where were the Germans? Why hadn't they taken the stricken city? Were they waiting for the fires to burn themselves out so they could dance on the embers in their jackboots? So they could march down the main street to cheers and bouquets from admirers – those cockroaches who'd crawl out of nooks and crannies when crumbs fell from German tables.

Tania gazed sadly at her city and its river, and a hard glint came into her eyes.

'NOT ONE STEP BACK!' she shouted.

All at once she felt ravenously hungry. She'd hardly eaten for five days.

In the kitchen she found some stale black bread as hard as a brick, a jar of pickled cucumbers with green mould on top and a few Antonov apples. A saucepan on the gas stove contained the remains of beetroot soup. It smelt sour.

'Needs must where Hitler drives,' she murmured, wrinkling her nose as she dipped a hard crust into the soup pot. Hungrily she tipped up the pot and drank the cold liquid, then chewed on sour cabbage, beetroot and bread, and sucked the remaining juice out of a knuckle-bone.

In the unplugged fridge was a jar of runny cherry

preserve and a half-bottle of soured cream. She ate that too.

Next on the agenda: a good wash and change of clothes. How she longed to soak in a hot bath, soap herself all over and clean the dirt out of her hair! No such luck. When Tania turned on the taps, all that dribbled out were rusty blobs. Luckily, there was some water left in the kettle, though no gas to heat it up. She made do with kettle-water to wash her hair and face, wiping the rest of her body down with the rough bundle of raffia the family used for washing.

When she looked at herself in the bathroom mirror, she scarcely recognised the little fair-haired girl with hazel eyes and what Dad called 'a peaches and cream complexion'. The face staring anxiously out at her was lined and bruised, the hair lank and singed, the bloodshot eyes ringed by dark circles. Swapping her dirty underwear for fresh, and her filthy, tattered fatigues for baggy ski pants and jumper, she stood before the mirror once more… and saluted.

'Gunner Tania Belova reporting for duty.'

Suddenly she had second thoughts.

No! She'd done her bit on guns. Now she could get back to nursing. After blowing people to pieces, it was time to put them back together again. She looked at the mirror and said quietly, 'Nurse Tania Belova, reporting for duty.'

Her smile faded as other thoughts forced a way in. Who was she to pick and choose? There was a war on.

All she could do was report to army headquarters and request medical duties.

Still unsteady on her feet, her head throbbing, her hands smarting, she limped out of the flat, leaving the door unlocked, just in case…

Outside, she asked passers-by where the nearest command post was. She was in luck. A young soldier pointed towards the river.

'They've taken over the old communist offices in Solechnaya, on the embankment.'

Thanking him, she walked the short distance to a tall, granite building halfway along the embankment. A sentry checked her identity and directed her to an office down the left-hand corridor. 'You'll find the recruiting office down there, lass,' he said.

There were uniformed men and women everywhere, bustling about, shouting instructions, poring over maps stuck to the walls beneath portraits of Lenin and Stalin. No one paid her any attention. Not far along the corridor she found a heavy door wide open.

Behind it, a shaven-headed, thick-set man with bushy black eyebrows and a face like a bull-dog was sitting at a huge desk, cigarette stuck in the corner of his mouth. Noticing her in the doorway, he shouted, without looking up, 'Yes?'

'Gunner Tatiana Belova,' she said quietly.

He snorted and looked up.

'Gunner? This isn't the artillery! It's the police. See this?' He tapped his green epaulettes. 'I'm

Major-General Rogatin, Commander of the 71st Special Service Company, River District.'

She apologised.

'I'm sorry, Comrade Major-General. I just wanted to report for duty.'

'What is your duty, soldier?' he asked.

'Anti-aircraft guns, Comrade Major-General. But I'd like to be a nurse.'

He sighed. 'Not our line. Try the clinic down the road.'

As she turned to go, he suddenly called out, 'Hold on a minute. Belova? You're not Ivan Belov's girl, by any chance?'

'Yes, Comrade Major-General.'

'Good God! I assigned your father myself: Commissar to Rodimtsev's army.'

He grinned, scratching the heavy stubble on his chin.

'Maybe I can use you. Look, I need a runner. I'm desperately short of men. Can I trust you to take something to your father? He's somewhere across the river. Bringing up reinforcements. Find him, give him this...'

He hesitated for a moment, drumming his fingers on the table and staring hard at the bruised girl before him. Was she old enough for such a dangerous mission?

'See here, Tania,' he said, looking down at his hands. 'German tanks are at the approach to the city Our only chance is help from across the Volga. You'll have to slip across at night, under cover of darkness.

46

Do you think you can do it?'

'Of course,' she murmured.

He handed her an oblong envelope.

'Guard it with your life.'

'Yes, Comrade Major-General,' she said, putting the envelope in her pocket. Nursing would have to wait... again. She smiled, thinking how surprised Dad would be to see her.

The officer's grim face cracked into a grin, showing a mouthful of iron teeth.

'Wait, girl. I'll write out a pass. Tatiana Belova... Date of birth?'

'Thirteenth of February, 1926.'

'Education?'

'Eight years.'

He wrote this down, stamped the pass and handed it over.

'You're one of us now, Chekistka.'

Chekistka? This was the old name for the Secret Police!

TWELVE

Suddenly, the full realisation of what Tania had become hit her. She was in the police: feared like the devil, hated like poison. But she couldn't refuse. She gulped and mumbled the stock army response,

'Glad to serve.'

'And kill?'

'Yes, Comrade Major-General,' she said smartly. 'Any Germans I can get my hands on.'

He shook his head.

'Not just Germans. We kill traitors, deserters, defeatists, cowards, spies, drunks, saboteurs, fifth columnists. Russian or German, makes no difference.'

She nodded, not quite understanding.

How do you tell a coward from a hero? Mum had said that a lot of innocent people had been sent to labour camps, some shot as spies and saboteurs. What if the police had overheard her? Tania needed to check and see if there was any signs of struggle at home.

'Report here when you get back,' Rogatin shouted after Tania as she walked dumbly from the office. 'Don't talk to a soul, and don't leave home till midnight.'

The thought of seeing Dad again lent wings to Tania's stiff, aching body. She wasn't sorry to get out of Stalingrad, but not if her mother and brothers were still here. She had to get home, to find any clues to their whereabouts.

From the yellow building on the embankment she walked slowly through the streets, braving bombs and shells and collapsing buildings. She had to clamber over rubble blocking the street, and avert her eyes from the wounded being seen to by nurses and doctors.

As she climbed the stairs to the flat, her heart beat fast. Would anyone be home? Perhaps Mum and her brothers were back, worried sick about her. She'd go in and they'd be sitting round the table, sipping tea and eating bread and cheese. 'Hello, Tanechka,' Mum would say with a big smile. 'Thank God you're safe.'

But, no: the flat was as silent as the grave. Just the wind blowing through the empty windows, making the curtains flap.

'Hello-o-oah!' she called.

Nothing.

She was alone, and scared. What if Germans came through the door? There was no Mum or Dad to stop them shooting her as a spy.

Tania sat on the edge of the sofa, and tears started in her eyes, overflowed and rolled down her cheeks. She didn't want to cry. She wanted to be brave, to stand up and show she wasn't afraid. But she cried tears of grief and shame.

From the corner of her seat she gazed through blurred eyes at the broken windows and crockery. Had the police or Germans come, and had Mum thrown plates and soup at them? If so, the wardrobe and chest-of-drawers would be open where they'd pulled out clothes in a hurry. But no, they were closed.

As she rummaged through the cupboards, however, Tania found that their warm coats and hats had gone. Did that mean they'd been evacuated somewhere safe, to the Urals perhaps? Her head spun with questions.

That's enough! Abruptly, she wiped away the tears and rubbed her eyes with grubby fists. She'd have gone to Mum's clinic if Rogatin hadn't told her to stay put until midnight. And she was to avoid contact with 'fifth columnists' – not that she could tell a fifth from a third or even a sixth columnist. Did they go around in columns of five?

She crunched her way over broken glass into the bedroom and, brushing the glass and plaster from the bed, lay down to rest. In no time at all she was fast asleep – and twisting her gun sights, pressing the firing button, shooting at enemy planes...

THIRTEEN

By the time Tania awoke it was dark, apart from red fires reflected in glass splinters on the floor. Cold air filled the room. The thunder of guns and shells rumbled on.

Alarmed, she peered at her watch in the half-light of the flares. It was 11 o'clock. Time to go!

Heart in her mouth, she took a torch from the hall-stand, hurried down the stairwell and out of the front door. It was a humid, moonless night; even the full moon couldn't pierce the black umbrella over the city. Out loud she quoted her favourite poet, Alexander Pushkin:

Storm-clouds whirl and storm-clouds scurry;
From behind them pale moonlight
Flickers where the snowflakes hurry.
Dark the sky and dark the night.

As she walked down the middle of the road to avoid falling masonry, she took stock of her situation. From schoolgirl to gunner to spy in just a few days. Dad would be proud of her, but Mum would be worried sick. As she thoughts turned to her mother, she grew sad: Mum would want her to heal the sick, not add to their numbers.

She picked her way down to the docks. There was no

motor launch to be seen; it had evidently been blown up that afternoon. Instead, a rowing boat was waiting, slapping its flat prow on the water and rocking up and down. She snapped on her torch for a moment to check.

The boat was white with a blue stripe down both sides and the number 7 painted in dark brown on the bows. Only days before, she could have rented it for a rouble an hour and rowed down the Volga.

Two men in olive-green uniform were sitting at the oars. They flicked on a flashlight to examine her pass. 'Can't be too careful,' one said, as the other examined the stamp on the pass. Satisfied, they grunted, indicating a place in the gunwales, then pushed off in silence.

It was a quiet night on the river, black sky above, black waters below. The Germans had stopped bombing. The *rat-tat-tat* of rifle fire could be heard in the distance, perhaps three or four kilometres away like a far-off rumble of thunder, so distant her ears paid scant attention.

She breathed in the swampy river smell and was engrossed in her thoughts, when a voice broke into her musings.

'How old are you, girl?' growled the nearer man, huddled in a greatcoat.

'Sixteen.'

'Oh yeah, and I'm sixty,' he muttered disbelievingly.

'Soon be on a pension then,' she muttered, irritated by his scornful tone.

'War ain't for little girls,' he said sullenly.

'If you can't stop the Germans, we girls will have to!' she said.

His mate gave a muffled chuckle.

'That's one in the eye for you, Kolya.'

They fell silent.

The crossing was eerie and unreal. The rowing boat passed a half-submerged barge rearing out of the water like some prehistoric sea-monster. As the water gently slapped the bows and the rowlocks creaked in unison, dull thumps of shell-bursts echoed hollowly in the river air.

At the far shore the boat nosed up to a jetty, like a dog to its master, and grated on the sand. The man closest to land leapt ashore and secured the boat with rope to a breakwater stump. The second motioned to Tania to wait, as he shipped the oars and hurried off into the night.

When he returned some twenty minutes later, he helped her from the boat and whispered in her ear, as if the enemy might hear three or four kilometres away, 'Rodimtsev's troops are about ten kilometres from here, in the hamlet of Nikitskoye. Our comrade will drive you there.'

Then, as an afterthought, he hissed, 'You should be at home with your dolls.'

His breath stank of garlic and vodka. Best to ignore him. All the same, Tania was angry inside. She was a gunner, after all; she'd shot down nine planes, she'd fought to defend her city.

'This way,' called an old fellow from above the bank. 'Prepare yourself for a bumpy ride.'

He led the way up the sandy bank to a shingle pathway. There stood a dusty old snub-nosed American Studebaker. The driver patted it fondly and said in English, 'Let's go, pardner.'

Tania took her seat, cast one last glance at the inferno she was leaving behind, sighed deeply and screwed her eyes tight. When she opened them, she didn't look back once.

FOURTEEN

As Tania bumped along in the car, she counted the days since school. It seemed light years away. Only last week she had been giggling at a Chekhov story, learning a Pushkin poem, loving Chukovsky's rhymes, skipping and playing hopscotch and tag. So much had happened in the blink of an eye. She'd swapped her brown school dress for dungarees, her shoes for boots, her skipping rope for a gun. What next? Grappling with Germans? It was too hard for a schoolgirl – whoops – new soldier to deal with.

The old driver, Timofei, was in no hurry. Ahead, the highway wandered off into the darkness, God knows where. It was too risky to shine a light. So driver and passenger bounced up and down, rocked from side to side – to Tania's groans and Timofei's curses, as the wheels hit ruts and pitched into craters. A pain shot up her back each time the car tossed her about. It felt like riding on a lumbering camel.

After some three kilometres the old man swung the wheel sharply, turning the car off towards a cluster of houses silhouetted against the sky. They passed a quaint wooden shack which looked for all the world like Baba Yaga's hut on hen's legs. On a distant hill, the white walls and onion dome of a church were reflected in the far-off firelight.

'No sense crocking her,' remarked the driver. 'We'll rest here till dawn.'

He pulled up by the church wall, alongside ghostly rows of lorries. Perhaps the church was being used as a storage dump.

If Tania thought they'd be alone inside the church, she was in for a shock. As they entered, she saw in the glimmer of candlelight that the place was packed with army men.

They were sitting or lying on the stone floor, huddled together, deathly pale and unshaven, blood-stained bandages showing up against dusty uniforms. Their dull eyes followed her as she edged round one side, stepping over still forms.

Crossing himself as he led the way, Timofei was heading for a door at the far end. It was painted with a gaunt image of Jesus Christ, long-faced and hollow-cheeked. The low doorway was in the centre of an icon-covered screen that separated the two parts of the church: one public, the other sacred. From the strong earthy smell, the place must recently have been a potato store; now it was a refuge for the sick and lame.

As she followed Timofei through the low door, to her surprise Tania saw more wounded packed together like a tin of sprats. But these were civilians, mostly women and children wrapped in dark grey hospital blankets.

'They're evacuating the city hospitals,' whispered Timofei.

Somehow the sight of wounded soldiers was not as

painful as this helpless mass. Tania kept her eyes fixed on the floor tiles before her, but there was so little space, she couldn't help bumping into an outstretched leg or stumbling over a writhing, groaning child. One woman had an infant at her breast; the child, his bald head pitted with black scars, must have been two or more; he sucked on his mother's teat for comfort, not food.

A nurse with long, tangled ginger hair was painting green iodine on a boy's open cheek wound, murmuring, 'Be a brave soldier', as he whimpered quietly. The mother beside him lay mouth open, eyes wide, arms reaching for the son she would no longer touch.

Amidst the low moans and sudden cries Tania heard someone calling her name. At first she thought she must be hearing things.

'Tania, is that you?'

Yes, there it was again. A girl's voice, faint and trembling.

As Tania's eyes grew accustomed to the gloom, she nervously searched the stretchers and bundles littering the floor

Who would know her here, in a distant village church? A shiver ran through her. Who was it?

'Tania.'

This time she pinpointed the sound. It was coming from close by, just two bodies away. No movement. No waving arm. No shake of the head. Just a tiny, mouse-like squeak. With a shock, Tania recognised the pale face framed in dark curls.

Nina!

A mixture of pain and fear gripped her. She spoke the first words that came into her head.

'How are you?'

Silence. Then a sniffle.

Hastily Tania asked another question: 'Where are they taking you?'

A pause, to summon a stream of breath.

'Beyond the Urals.'

'Good, you'll be safe there.'

To herself, she thought darker thoughts: only if we hold the German army at Stalingrad.

Comforted by Tania's presence, Nina fell silent. Tania, meanwhile, eased herself into the space cleared by Timofei and nibbled on the rusks he took from his pocket. She sank back and closed her eyes. Her mind kept re-running old pictures of Nina – skating in a fluffy tutu skirt on the frozen river, slim and graceful as she danced on the school stage, playing a squeaky violin at a club concert... She'd never skate, dance or play again. What would become of her?

'See you in the morning, Nina,' Tania said gently, tears flowing down her cheeks.

There was no reply.

FIFTEEN

Nina didn't see her in the morning, for Tania and Timofei were already chugging along the highway to the dawn chorus of birdsong. The early glimmer of daylight helped the driver steer a passage between pot-holes and the deepest ruts, and soon they were beyond shell and mortar holes. Now and then a bomb crater loomed ahead, forcing them on to a grass verge. Or a wrecked truck blocked the way. Or a column of slow-moving refugee lorries jammed the road.

The skilful driver overtook them all, his gnarled hand jammed on the horn. No doubt the slower vehicles thought he was driving some army bigwig – maybe reporting to Stalin himself – not a slip of a girl with raggedy corn-coloured pigtails who'd wandered into the Secret Police by mistake.

For the first time Tania was able to take a good look at her companion. He was old, well over seventy. His face was lined with countless deep wrinkles, like a sun-baked prune. His straggly grey beard dangled halfway down his chest. Although he was wearing an unbuttoned army jacket, underneath was an old-fashioned black waistcoat and a relatively clean, homespun shirt.

He hummed cheerfully to himself.

'Aren't you scared, Granddad?' she suddenly asked.

He gave the question some thought before replying.

'Me? No!'

Then he had second thoughts, for he spoke slowly, staring straight ahead.

'Well, I'm not scared of shells or bombs or bullets – I got used to all that in the last war. No, the scariest thing about war is silence, when you're doing nothing, when you don't know what's going on. It's far worse sitting in a trench than it is charging forward. In a trench you can only sit there counting the bombs, wondering whether your name's on one.'

He broke off to hoot his horn at stragglers ahead, blocking the road. Then he continued, this time in sombre mood.

'We'll all die soon enough, anyway. Death is what war's about, isn't it? I've had my time, I don't mind dying.'

Tania said nothing. She hadn't had her time. She did mind dying. It mattered a lot, and not just to her. To Mum and Dad, to her friends. She trembled at the thought of being blown to bits, so that no one could put her together again, no one would know where she was or how she had died.

They drove along in silence. Then, Timofei said something that unnerved Tania.

'What's the use of fighting?'

He was combing the tangled beard with his left hand.

'Fritz has come all the way from Berlin to Stalingrad in his Panzers and Messers, with his Nebelwerfer launchers and machine-guns. And what do we have to stop him? –

an old 1890 model rifle, like this one here.' He jerked a thumb towards his rifle.

Tania wanted to object. It was her patriotic duty to prevent such defeatist talk. And she was a Chekistka now; she could report him at the next road block, have him shot.

Part of her felt important and powerful, keen to report traitors to the authorities. But these zealous thoughts were soon swallowed up by others: she wasn't a tell-tale, let alone a toady for the Secret Police. She didn't want old Timofei shot.

'We don't know how to fight a modern war,' he continued bitterly.

'What do you mean, we don't know how?' she said, her voice rising.

'Like I said: the Germans have managed to get from Berlin to the Volga – that takes some doing.'

'Well,' she retorted, 'the Red Army have retreated all the way to the Volga... that takes some doing too!'

He laughed a dry, scornful laugh.

Tania was bewildered. She'd never met anyone like him before: unafraid, straight-talking. Everyone else put a brave face on things, had no doubts who would win. Yet here was this old man asking, 'What's the use of fighting?'

She didn't agree. She couldn't agree. But she couldn't help wondering to herself whether he was right...

SIXTEEN

As the morning opened up, so did enemy guns. Although the Studebaker was now out of range of mortar shells from the far side of the Volga, the skies posed other threats.

Tania gazed at the innocent sky: beautiful, blue, cloudless, the most summery sky imaginable – just the weather for sunbathing on the sand, eating ice cream, playing leap-frog. In peacetime it would be a perfect summer's day. But it was a merciless killer in war, offering no hiding place.

If only a cloud would appear.

If only a shower of rain would fall.

If only fog or mist would descend.

'Give me autumn mud and storm clouds,' muttered Timofei between clenched teeth.

The sky was filled with sinister black planes. All day long Messerschmitts buzzed through the air like angry bees, patrolling the highway in pairs, firing their bullets at defenceless convoys. Now and then they'd drop shiny little bombs – two to a wing, four to a plane, sometimes long cigar boxes that rattled in the air as they tumbled over and over.

'Watch out for those rattlers,' warned Timofei. 'They're full of grenades that scatter far and wide, like hailstones.' He gave a humourless laugh. 'Soldiers do their washing in them – the two halves make handy troughs.'

Whenever German planes appeared, Timofei drove off the road to shelter in a clump of trees. The trucks driving in the opposite direction, taking reinforcements to Stalingrad, were in too much of a hurry to take cover; the many wrecked vehicles along the wide road testified to the price paid to save Stalingrad. Here and there, the dusty track was patterned by little squares and triangles from tyre treads where wounded drivers had lost control and skewed their trucks round.

After one raid, as the car regained the bullet-mown highway, Tania noticed a bizarre sight: a broken signpost run down by a lorry lay in the middle of the road, its one arm pointing skywards. It declared:

STALINGRAD 8 KM.

'Not far to Heaven,' remarked Timofei, with a humourless grin.

Early that morning, in the first rays of the sun, Ilyushin dive-bombers had passed overhead, furiously screeching. Now they were on their way back, tails between their legs. Tania could see their fuselages full of holes, and flying so low, they were almost touching the treetops with their wheels. Less than half were coming back.

Meanwhile, the mighty Messerschmitts could be seen

in the distance, circling over the Volga like carrion crows. Here and there, black mushrooms of smoke were rising into the air from burning aeroplanes.

Tania craned her neck until it hurt to follow the air battles. Small and black, high above, the planes twisted and turned, and sometimes spiralled downwards, trailing smoke as they fell.

Timofei had the keen eye and ear of a hunter. He could tell an MIG from a Messerschmitt at any height.

'You can tell by the sound,' he explained. 'Now, take our little U-2 biplanes. In the distance they remind you of a sewing machine – *clickety-click, clackety-clack*. Then, as they approach the target, the pilots switch off their engines and glide in, air rushing through the struts; it sounds like wild swans swishing their wings. Since their bomb load is only light, it drops like peas from a pod: *plop-plop-plop*. That's our noise.

'The Stuka dive-bombers sing a different song. Soldiers call them "screamers" or "musicians" because of their wailing sirens. When they go into a dive, pilots switch on sirens attached to the wings. At first, they scared the living daylights out of us because we used to think they were screaming bombs.'

Tania listened to what old Timofei said. If she ever had to go back to her guns, this knowledge would come in useful.

After another couple of kilometres, Timofei muttered, 'Not far now.'

The only sign of habitation was the occasional

farmhouse or fisherman's cottage: isolated, mostly deserted. Outside one wayside shack an old woman was standing in the dust, gazing forlornly at the passing trucks. Her own transport stood in the yard: three tethered camels shaking their large ugly heads and looking round in alarm. These ships of the steppe seemed as out of place in the theatre of war as the white storks nesting in her straw roof.

SEVENTEEN

Tania saw a cloud of dust in the distance; the air had become heavy and troubled, and she could hear a low rumbling.

'That's a 37-millimetre anti-aircraft gun,' she informed her companion.

He looked at her in surprise. 'Are you sure?'

'Oh, yes. I used to fire one myself.'

He smiled grimly.

Up ahead was what looked like a military camp, bristling with long-barrelled guns pointing skywards and MIG fighter planes circling overhead, ready to drive off invading Stukas and Messers.

They had to pass three road blocks before being allowed through. Each time, the guards smiled knowingly at the occupants of the Studebaker, as if they all belonged to some special club.

'They're ours,' said Timofei.

By which he meant not Russian, but Secret Police.

And she was one of them. A Chekistka. Was she privileged to be one of the chosen? She'd never pulled wings off moths or stamped on ants. Killing Germans, OK, if it meant shooting in self-defence, for Mother Russia. But killing your own people? No, she could never do that.

Suddenly, unexpectedly, it started raining. Not a light summer shower, but a torrential downpour. By the time they arrived at the last check-point, at about ten o'clock, there were puddles everywhere and the sentries were soaked to the skin. 'Almost there now,' Tania thought excitedly. If she shouted out, her dad might hear her. Her heart beat faster.

After checking their papers, an officer stood on the tailboard, waving soldiers out of the way and guiding them to a delicately-carved wooden house in the middle of the camp.

'Hand me your report,' he ordered. 'I'll take it to Commissar Belov.'

Tania sat tight.

'I was told to deliver it myself,' she said apologetically.

'This isn't a child's game,' he retorted angrily. 'I'm an officer, I'm in charge here.'

She wasn't certain what to do.

Then a familiar voice bailed her out.

'No, I'm in charge here, Captain. My daughter is obeying the orders of Major-General Rogatin.'

The Army Captain looked daggers at Tania. But he said nothing. It was clear there was no love lost between the army and the police. He turned away, pulling up his coat collar against the driving rain.

Tania's father was standing in the doorway of the log cabin, a cigarette in the corner of his mouth, one eye screwed up against the smoke, the other giving his daughter a broad wink. Short and stocky, he reminded her of a rock, rough-hewn and steadfast. He had an air of calm authority about him; his speech, like his movements, were unhurried. Hands deep in the pockets of a black leather jacket, he walked slowly down the wooden steps into the rain and hugged her tight.

Tania was a little girl again in her father's arms. She smiled happily as she smelled the familiar strong tobacco in his wiry hair and leather jacket, and felt the rough stubble of his chin against her cheek.

'I heard you were coming on the field telephone,' he said, pulling her up the steps out of the rain. 'Thank God you made it safely. What's new on the home front?'

'The flat's a mess,' she said guardedly.

His face darkened.

'You mean?'

'No, no. There's no sign of anyone, no blood or struggle or anything. I bumped into a girl who's being evacuated. Probably Mum and the boys are on their way to safety too. I hope they are.' Her voice was anxious.

He breathed a sigh of relief that travelled all the way up from his boots.

'That makes sense,' he muttered.

An orderly brought two enamel mugs of tea and set them down on the oilskin table-cloth, with two small lumps of sugar each. For some time they sat, father and daughter, sipping tea in silence, each holding a lump of sugar in their teeth and sucking tea through it.

EIGHTEEN

With a sigh, her father carefully brushed crumbs from the table.

'Well, how's life?' he said. 'Eh, Tanechka?'

'OK,' she said quietly.

'Everything's a mess, isn't it? Never mind, it'll right itself soon. What have you been up to?'

'Nothing really, Dad. I shot down nine enemy planes...'

As she told him of the Pioneer brigade, of her anti-aircraft assignment, of the chance meeting with Rogatin, his eyes grew wide.

'What? My little girl? A hero... Unbelievable.'

He stood up and pulled her head to his chest, stroking her fair hair, gently feeling the bump and cut on her scalp. All the while, he was murmuring, 'Tanechka, my ballerina, my little nurse... my soldier, a killer...'

She swung away in horror.

'I'm not a killer!' she exclaimed. 'I didn't mean to kill anyone. I had no choice.'

He smiled sadly.

'Yes, yes, I know. None of us have a choice. We didn't want this war. But we can't defend ourselves without killing the enemy, can we?'

He sat down again. As Tania continued to sip her tea,

he ripped open the buff envelope and read the single sheet of paper inside, front and back.

'Mmmm... No... The devil! Mmmm...'

Looking up, he muttered, 'Could be worse.'

Now it was her turn to shrug, not knowing what the note said.

'Let's go,' he said abruptly.

'Where to?' she asked, surprised.

'To report to General Rodimtsev.'

'Who's he?'

'Our Commander-in-Chief.'

'Oh,' she said, puzzled. 'I thought you were in charge.'

For the first time he relaxed, laughing heartily.

'I'm only an old stoker from Stalingrad! But give me time...'

'And I'm only a little schoolgirl who wants to be a nurse,' she said. 'Funny how things change, all at once, without giving you time to breathe. Your thoughts don't keep up. I keep waking up and thinking I'm late for school. But then my brain switches on and I'm in the middle of a war.'

Her father smiled sadly.

'I know what you mean, Tanechka. It seems only yesterday you were bossing your brothers about, flirting with that lad Alyosha...'

'I never did!' she cried, feeling herself blushing.

Her dad roared with laughter.

NINETEEN

The Division's command post was in a cellar of the village council offices. You could be forgiven for thinking the windowless ruin was deserted: above ground there was no sign of life. But below beat the pulse of the army command.

As Tania followed her father down narrow wooden steps, she suddenly found herself in a gallery hacked out of stony clay and reinforced by wooden pillars and beams. The floor was a mixture of beaten earth and planks bridging narrow gullies of brackish water flowing through the cellar. Smoky oil lamps provided patchy light for those who needed it, to see their maps and reports and operate the telephones. Elsewhere, most of the gallery lay in dark shadow.

A female wireless operator was babbling away, repeating over and over in a high-pitched voice, 'Come in, this is Moon. This is Moon.'

Other operators, mostly men, were squatting in corners, holding foul-smelling cigarettes in their fists and trying not to let the smoke drift towards the officers. The *mahorka* weed mingled with stale sweat, stinking mud and a suffocating stuffiness that made Tania gasp.

As her eyes, ears and nose grew accustomed to the atmosphere, she realised that this lamp-lit underworld was linked to Stalingrad's factories and mills, to its dug-outs, trenches and gun batteries, to front-line command posts and river jetties.

The man holding the threads was sitting on an upturned box with an American eagle stamped on the side. His head was bent low over a vast map of Stalingrad, resting on several smaller maps lying upon a trestle table. His hair was iron grey, shorn at the sides and standing up like a stiff bristle broom, making his head look chimney-shaped – Tania almost expected smoke to rise up at any moment.

So this was General Alexander Rodimtsev, Hero of the Soviet Union!

As she stood behind her father, waiting for the General to look up, Tania suddenly felt the floor, walls and ceiling shake and heave from bombs exploding. Phones jangled, orange lamp-flames jigged up and down, and eerie shadows shuddered their way across the earthen walls.

Tania froze. What if the roof tumbled in, burying them all? Like Nina – lying under tons of earth, unable to breathe or move a muscle, in total darkness and silence, slowly, oh so slowly suffocating to death.

Yet the underground 'moles' went about their work as if nothing had happened. Rodimtsev, too, didn't bat an eyelid, calmly continuing to issue instructions.

'Well, Commissar?' he said, without glancing up. 'What news from Stalingrad?'

Tania's father stepped forward and saluted as best he could in the low room.

'Police report, Comrade Commander.' He put the buff envelope on the table.

The General's long fingers pulled out the sheet. His grey eyes scanned it swiftly.

'Hmm, same old story,' he muttered to himself. 'Same as the army report.'

Looking up, he said, 'Not so good, eh?'

'Could be worse, Comrade General.'

'Oh, yes. And it will be worse before it gets better. They've got to hold out until we arrive.'

'Any order from Moscow?' Tania's dad asked.

'Only to stay put. We can't move until the Sixty-Second Army is ready on all fronts.' He glanced about him with an exasperated look. 'While the orchestra's tuning up, Stalingrad burns. Still, we need every instrument to play in tune and settle into the rhythm of battle. Then we'll play our battle symphony: bang the drums, sound the horns, roar out a victory march...'

All at once, he noticed Tania.

'Hey, you, girl! You're not a German spy, are you?' he said with a grin.

Tania stepped forward and saluted smartly, red in the face.

'I'm a Stalingradka, Comrade General,' she said indignantly. 'I brought the report from Major-General Rogatin.'

His eyes twinkled and he smiled broadly.

'So, you delivered the report, eh? Dangerous mission. What's your name?'

'Tatiana Belova, Comrade Commander.'

His thick black eyebrows rose a fraction.

'I see. Like father, like daughter, eh? Well, now you're here, we must find work for you. Report back tomorrow morning at 08.00.'

Tania felt a thrill of excitement as she saluted.

TWENTY

All the time General Rodimtsev was talking, the phones kept ringing non-stop. Without taking his eyes off Tania and her father, he turned his head slightly, issuing curt orders to the duty staff officer, listening to reports and giving replies.

Fumbling in a box beneath the table, the General brought up a tin of meat. He held it up to the light: on all sides were pictures of different dishes to be made from corned beef.

'Canned in Chicago,' he read, as he broke off the opener soldered to the bottom of the tin. He threaded the tin's lip through the eye of the opener and peeled off the lid. With a penknife, he cut the red-and-white-speckled meat into three equal chunks.

'Trust our Allies to make meat the same colour as their flag! Here – dig in, you Belovs. You deserve a reward.'

Tania hadn't eaten since early morning at the church, yet it didn't seem right to be seen enjoying such privileges.

'No, thank you,' she said. 'I'm not hungry.'

He smiled, wrapping her portion in newspaper, and handed it to her.

'Eat it later when you feel hungry – and that's an order.'

It was also a dismissal.

Tania followed her father back to his quarters and, after sharing a meal of corned beef, black bread and raw onion, she lay down on a bunk in the corner. It wasn't long before she was fast asleep.

***

By the time she woke up, her father had gone. A note pinned to the table told her he'd had to leave on an urgent mission. *See you soon, Tanechka*, the note ended.

It was time to freshen up. Now she was a soldier, she had to look her smartest for the General. The rain-barrel in the yard provided water for her face and hands; she rubbed her teeth with a finger dipped in salt and did her best to plait her tangled hair. Then, brushing herself down, she set off for the underground command post.

What job would the General have for her? There must surely be a need for nurse. At last she'd have her wish. She wondered whether he'd send her back to Stalingrad; that was probably where Dad was headed.

On the stroke of eight she was standing in front of the General's desk. He was waiting, already shaven, though with the same crumpled jacket and trousers. His first words took her by surprise.

'Grip my hand. Hard!'

Tania hesitated.

'Go on, I won't bite it off,' he said, putting a long-fingered hand on the table.

She took his hand: it was twice the size of hers, but surprisingly soft and warm.

'Now, give it a strong handshake.'

He was obviously testing her for something. But what? She grasped his hand firmly and held it for a full minute.

'Right,' he said, taking his hand away. He stared at her long and hard before speaking, half to himself.

'Your grip is firm, hand's steady. How's your eyesight?'

She frowned. 'Good, Comrade General.'

Then she couldn't help herself; she blurted out, 'Good enough to shoot down nine German planes – so they tell me. I was four days on anti-aircraft guns.'

He whistled through his teeth and raised his bushy eyebrows.

'You don't say! What's your favourite subject at school?'

She thought a bit.

'Physics.'

'Good. Did you do optics?'

'Ye-e-sss. Studying light through lenses.'

'What's an optic axis?'

Oh dear – if this was a test, she was about to fail. She was silent.

'An optic axis,' he explained like a schoolmaster, 'is a line passing through the centre of a lens or spherical mirror, parallel to the axis of symmetry.'

He sat back in his chair, occasionally glancing at the young girl before him. At last he spoke, more to himself than to her.

'Firm hand, keen eye, handy with guns.' Then, 'How do you fancy becoming a sniper?'

Sniper? What a strange-sounding word, thought Tania. What do snipers do? Snipe at each other? Shoot snipe…?

TWENTY-ONE

Tania sat in puzzled silence.

'The battle to come,' said the General, looking keenly at her, 'will be like no other in history. We'll be fighting for every house, every flat, every bunker, every cellar, every sewer. And high up in the ruined buildings, snipers with telescopic sights and steady hands will be watching the enemy – like eagles from their eyries.

'The Germans aren't used to close combat. It goes against their orderly nature. But we Russians are natural hunters – of foxes, wolves, bears. Picking off Germans will be child's play.'

Tania wanted to say she'd never hunted in her life – never even shot at sparrows from a catapult. But she said nothing.

'With your steady hand, you'll make a first-class sniper,' he went on. 'I've just set up a sniper school – about a dozen youngsters under Lieutenant Zaitsev. You'll meet them on the rifle range. Any questions?'

'No, Comrade Commander. Glad to serve.'

She saluted, turned about and, after receiving directions for the rifle range, left the command post.

Well, well, she thought, life is full of surprises.

She couldn't help feeling confused. She'd set her heart on nursing and now, here she was – a sniper. A tingle of excitement ran right through her, from the ends of her pigtails to the tips of her toe-nails.

Yet, as she hurried along the muddy path towards the rifle range, she thought, 'Slow down. Not so fast.'

It was one thing shooting shells into the sky, hoping to hit a distant metal blob before it dropped its bombs. Even though she had shot down nine planes, she hadn't seen the men fall out of the sky. So she couldn't say she'd actually killed anyone.

But a sniper... From what the General had said, snipers killed in cold blood. Sit, wait, train their sights on someone, pull the trigger... and hit him right between the eyes. No time to ask who he was, what he did, what he thought of war, did he have a family (maybe a daughter like her, with freckles and pigtails). He might be a stoker like her dad, forced to fight for his country. There wouldn't be time to ask questions.

Her steps were faltering now. Maybe she ought to turn back and say, 'Sorry, I want to be a field nurse.' She knew what he'd say in reply: 'Orders are orders. This is war. Life or death. It's them or us...'

She'd arrived at a low stone hangar covered in camouflage netting. Showing her pass, she went in.

Against the far wall someone had painted helmets and outlines of human figures. At the opposite end an instructor was standing over trainees, teaching them shooting techniques. She wasn't the only girl present; there were three others, out of fourteen.

The instructor came over. He was short and stocky

with high cheekbones and an open, honest face. His light brown hair had a little tuft at the front, as if he wanted to look taller. What struck her were his dark brown eyes – they seemed to bore right into her soul, making her heart flutter.

'Hello,' he said quietly, shaking her hand. 'Lieutenant Zaitsev – Vasily Ivanovich Zaitsev.'

'Tania Belova,' she said timidly.

'Ever handled a rifle?'

When she shook her head, he nodded matter-of-factly towards a store in the far corner. She was obviously not the first recruit who'd never held a rifle, let alone fired one.

'Go and sign for a rifle. Familiarise yourself with it and, when you're ready, we'll do some shooting practice.'

If the instructor was easy on her, the old quartermaster was surly and unhelpful. He soon made it clear he didn't hold with girl soldiers.

'Here's your rifle. Not too heavy, is it? Don't drop it on your foot. Sign here.'

She duly signed the form.

'How does it work?' she asked innocently.

'Eh? You're joking, aren't you? This is a sniper training course, not a kindergarten.'

As he was speaking, he read her name on the form, and a sudden note of respect crept into his voice when he realised she was the Commissar's daughter.

'Come, I'll show you,' he said gruffly.

For the next hour, the old quartermaster identified

the different parts, showing how to hold the rifle steady and press the trigger.

'Push the butt hard into your right shoulder,' he said. 'Place your left hand under the barrel, like so. Hold it steady and, with the right index finger, gently squeeze – don't pull – the trigger – as if you're coaxing milk from a goat's udder.'

Though Tania had never milked a goat, she knew what he meant. By lunchtime she had more or less got the hang of it. She lay on the stone floor, pressed the rifle into her shoulder, lined up the target and squeezed the trigger. To her surprise, the shots grew closer and closer to the black dot in the centre of the target. Within an hour of touching a rifle for the first time, all ten shots were puncturing the three inner rings.

She felt proud of herself. This was fun. But it wasn't meant to be fun. She might be good at it; that didn't mean she wanted to be a sniper. Hand and eye said one thing, head said another. Loud and clear, her brain screamed: I can't kill in cold blood! It went against all she'd learned at school: all men are brothers, all women sisters, the world over. Surely not all Germans are evil?

She gazed at the other trainees and wondered what they thought. Perhaps some had no qualms about shooting people. Maybe some had their doubts. She needed to know.

TWENTY-TWO

Tania soon came to know her comrades well. She made friends with a girl from a town called Berdichev. Lena was shy and timid; you could see it in her deep black eyes. They never looked straight at you, but darted all over the place. At the slightest mention of Germans, her eyes filled with hatred and she'd glance away. No one worked as hard as she did – shooting occupied her night and day.

'Is your family safe?' Tania asked one night, as they lay in neighbouring bunks.

Lena was silent for a long while. 'Do you know Berdichev?' she finally said.

'No.'

'It's a *stetl*.'

'What's that?'

'A Jewish settlement.'

'Oh.'

All at once, it dawned on Tania. She'd heard that the Germans hated Jews. If they'd captured Lena's town… It didn't bear thinking about.

Lena must have read her thoughts.

'Yes the Germans made straight for Berdichev. They're there now. So is – was – my family, all except Dad; he's at the front.'

She gulped down a sob.

'Do you know what they did? They marched all the Jews to a field outside town – thirty thousand of them – made them dig their own graves, then shot every single one, man, woman and child. No one survived.'

'What about you?'

'I was staying with an aunt in Kiev, so I escaped… The news came just before I was drafted to Stalingrad.'

Lena turned her face into her pillow.

Tania asked no more questions. But her friend's pain laid bare her own fears. She assumed her father was back in Stalingrad, but what of her mother and brothers? Could they be hiding in the sewers – amidst the filth and poisonous fumes? If so, they'd have to come up for air, like seals in the ocean. And once they popped up their heads…

It was more than Tania could bear to think of. At sixteen, part of her was still a little girl missing her mum. This time the little girl won. Tania buried her face in the pillow and cried like a baby.

***

The fourteen trainee snipers lived, ate and studied cheek by jowl. Night-time was the only time they were apart: the four girls shared bunks in a small store-room, and the ten men slept on a shed floor. They all shared the 'long drop' latrine in the yard and the drinking water in the rain-catcher holder hanging from an apple tree. They took turns cooking rations issued by the stingy quartermaster.

As Tania studied her new friends, she kept asking herself, over and over: what makes a sniper?

Each member of the team was different in so many ways – some shy and gentle, others rough and boastful. Yet they were all being trained to kill with a single shot. It was a subject they never talked about; most banished the thought from their minds.

The young instructor, Lieutenant Zaitsev, fascinated Tania. He never raised his voice. In fact, he hardly ever spoke more than a few words. He just touched an elbow, crooked a finger, straightened a back, tilted a head to one side. Or he'd demonstrate how to stalk like a leopard through undergrowth or rubble, his rifle strapped to his back.

Most important, he'd show them how to kill with a single bullet. 'You may only have one chance. Kill or be killed.'

Zaitsev taught them to shoot at stationary and moving targets, at flitting shadows, at different distances: ten, twenty, fifty, a hundred, two hundred metres. He told them which part of the body to aim at, how many centimetres to left or right, above or below the target, in wind, rain or snow.

He showed them how to use telescopic sights, which 'hide' to use to conceal the flash and smoke of a shot, how to judge distance by sight. On finishing the lesson, he'd always ask the same question:

'Am I right?'

They'd shout in chorus, 'Right, Vasily Ivanovich. Right.'

At that he'd give a faint smile, then urge them to go away and practise more.

TWENTY-THREE

Lena told Tania that Zaitsev had learned to fire a gun at the age of nine, as a shepherd in the summer pastures of the Ural Mountains. For weeks on end he had been guarding sheep and goats, alone, in the open, with only a rusty old rifle to ward off packs of hungry wolves. In wintertime he'd accompanied his father deep into Siberia's snowy fir and pine forests, hunting deer and wild boar; that's where he'd learned his hunting skills. When war came he was recruited as a rifleman – shooting Germans instead of wolves. Being able to shoot a running deer at two hundred paces was invaluable in wartime: so he was sent to Stalingrad.

And now he found himself in charge of a rag-taggle band that everyone called *zaichata* –- 'Zaitsev's kids'.

The team included a couple of experienced snipers from the Don and south-western fronts. Now that the Germans had overrun their positions, they'd been despatched to Stalingrad. One was a jolly, sandy-haired Ukrainian whom everyone called Salami. He was a few years older than the rest, sported a drooping, straw-coloured moustache and wore his cap at a jaunty angle. He liked nothing better than to talk of his war exploits.

'Well, it's like this, chaps. When I was at the front,

I accounted for five Fritzes in three days. Not bad, eh? Only another thirty-five and I'll be "Merited Sniper Salami".

'Anyway, this was my trick. I'd dig two false trenches on either side of me. Then I'd rig up a string of white flags and tin cans tied to cords in both trenches. When I pulled a cord – *Pop!* Up jumped my flags and cans. As soon as Fritz saw the flags waving or heard the cans rattling, he'd poke up his head for a better look, and he'd call out, "*Komm, Russ. Russ, komm hier!*" Up I'd jump and knock his block off. "That's for calling us Russians!" I'd yell. "I'm Ukrainian!"'

Everyone laughed at Salami's stories, though not entirely convinced of his claims.

What no one suspected was Tania's own war tally. It was General Rodimtsev who let the cat out of the bag during one of his daily inspections.

'Did you know, *zaichata*,' he said, 'you have a crack shot among you, someone who brought down nine enemy aircraft?'

The team was astonished, wondering who on earth the hero could be. The last person anyone suspected was little Tania Belova.

'Tatiana is a veteran of Stalingrad,' continued the General. 'She remained at her post for over four days and nights.'

Tania blushed to the roots of her hair as everyone stared at her.

From then on, Tania was looked upon with new

respect. Not that she welcomed the attention. Dark-eyed Lena seemed to look to her to avenge her family. Tania's greatest admirer, however, was a young man four years older than her. A more surprising candidate for sniping would be hard to find. Tolya Chekhov had bushy eyebrows, kind blue eyes and a stubborn chin; he came from Tatar lands on the River Kama.

'My favourite subject at school was geography,' he told Tania one day, as they were training in the forest. 'I dreamed of discovering woolly mammoths in the Siberian ice, or charting a new passage through the Arctic, or finding goldfields in Kamchatka. But Dad abandoned us when I was fourteen, and I had to quit school and earn a living.

'I soon became a jack-of-all-trades: mechanic, gas welder, fitter, electrician, builder, decorator; you name it, I did it.'

'How come you were chosen to be a sniper?' Tania asked. She knew he was bottom of the class in target practice.

Tolya laughed. 'God knows! I'd never harmed a hair on a caterpillar's back. I always felt sick at the sight of blood. I even used to rescue injured birds and care for them until they could fly again. I never imagined hurting a living creature, let alone shooting to kill. I suppose I'm just lucky.'

But Tolya's luck soon ran out. One evening he came to Tania looking down in the mouth. Some newcomers had arrived. Zaitsev had weeded out a student or two to make way for the new recruits – and Chekhov had scored a miserable nine out of fifty on the rifle range.

'I've been kicked out,' he said. 'Zaitsev says I'll never make a sniper.'

Tania felt sorry for him.

'What are you going to do?'

She imagined he'd be assigned to other duties – driver or sapper.

He screwed up his eyes.

'What am I going to do? Nothing. At least, nothing different. I'm going to prove them wrong.'

He lowered his voice, changing the tone.

'Tania, will you help me? I can't do it by myself.'

'What do you want me to do?' she asked in surprise.

'Teach me how to shoot. Help me become as good as you.'

She felt like saying, 'Shooting's like art or maths; if you don't have the gift, do something else. Go back to mending cars or tanks.'

Instead, she nodded dumbly.

TWENTY-FOUR

For a while Tolya was allowed to stay. Mostly he worked alone, reading up on theory for hours at a stretch. He got Tania to test him, asking him questions and checking his answers. Every day – morning, noon and night – she'd go with him to the forest where he'd train to determine distance by sight.

'How far is it to that larch?' he'd ask. And while he looked away, she'd pace out the distance.

'Is it fifty paces?' he asked.

'No.'

'Sixty?'

'No, you're a long way out.'

'Eighty-five?'

'No, it's forty-three.'

Slowly but surely, with Tania's help, he improved until he could work out distances by sight to within two or three metres.

Tolya taught himself to see landscape and elusive shadows as markers – silver birch trees, rose-hip bushes, lofty larches, red-berried mountain ash, even an old windmill they stumbled upon. In his mind, they were all places of danger where the enemy might be lurking. In no time at all he'd plot the distance, spin the fly-wheel of his range-finder and fire – accurately, with rarely an error.

'Well done, Tolya!' Tania would shout, clapping his good shots. 'You'll make a crack shot yet.'

Whenever she could, she'd give advice on holding the rifle steady, lining up the target, squeezing the trigger gently, unhurriedly – counting to five. Even when Tolya was posted to another unit as motor mechanic, they'd meet in the trees before dusk and practise some more.

One evening, when they were sitting on a log beneath a spreading larch, she voiced aloud her thoughts about killing.

'At school I was taught to love people, all people, no matter what their country. It's hard to switch to hate overnight.'

'I know what you mean, Tania,' he murmured.

Both sat in silence, thinking their own thoughts. It was so peaceful in the forest with just the birds chattering and the bees humming. The ash-grey leaves of the stately silver birch rustled in the breeze, and some way off a twig snapped under the foot of a hare or wild pig.

Tolya pulled a newspaper cutting from inside his jacket. He started to read:

'Let us not speak,
Let us not get angry,
Let us just kill.
If you don't kill a German,
He'll kill you…'

A hush came over them both.

'All I'm saying is that we're not like the Germans, brought up to hate. We must change, mustn't we?'

She remained silent, thinking of the last two lines of the poem:

'If you don't kill a German,
He'll kill you...'

Yes, she thought, and your mother, and your father, and your brothers.

'Thank you, Tolya,' she said, leaning over and kissing his cheek.

'What's that for?' he asked, surprised.

'You've helped me as much as I've helped you.'

***

About a month after he'd been with his new unit, Tolya turned up at the rifle range day, asking Zaitsev for another test. The sniper chief gave him three bullets.

'Rapid fire at fifty metres. Two out of three hits.'

Tania gave Tolya a confident smile as he lay on his stomach, and he breathed in deeply, as she'd taught him. Then he fired three times. She could see his lips counting – one, two, three, four, five – between shots.

He registered three hits right on the button.

Zaitsev was astonished. 'I was wrong,' he admitted candidly. 'You've done better than any other trainee. Good work!'

'Thank you, Vasily Ivanovich,' said Tolya, loud enough for Tania to hear. 'If it hadn't been for Tania, I'd never have done it.' And he gave her a grateful smile.

Tolya had made it just in time. At last the 62nd Army under General Chuikov was ready to ride to Stalingrad's rescue.

It was time for the sniper team to test their skills on real targets.

TWENTY-FIVE

A month after she had arrived at divisional headquarters, Tania was on the move again, this time travelling in the opposite direction. She was going home, but not to her mother and brothers – she'd had no news, but hopefully they were beyond the reach of German planes. Their continued safety, however, depended on the Red Army: the Germans must be stopped from crossing the Volga.

'Are you looking forward to going back?' Lena asked.

'Aren't you?' Tania said, forgetting for a moment the tragedy of Berdichev.

Lena thought for a bit before replying,

'No, not to an empty house.'

Tania bit her tongue. Then she said firmly, 'Yes. I'm glad to be going home, if only to make things safe for my mother and brothers to come back to.'

'Aren't you scared?' Lena asked, swiftly adding, 'I know I am.'

'I guess so. I'm scared about what we have to do. I don't want to die, but I do sometimes wonder how I'll feel about killing in cold blood.'

'Think what the Germans did to the Berdichev Jews,' Lena muttered.

'I will, Lenochka, I will.'

What sort of home awaited her? Tania wondered how

the city would look after forty days of bombardment. It was like a boxer on the ropes, unable to defend himself, pummelled by a gang of bruisers. But, miracle of miracles, the boxer was still on his feet, bloodied but not bowed. And now he was fighting back: the defenders of Stalingrad were holding on.

The Germans hadn't been able to take the city, nor cross the Volga, nor break through to the Urals. The Red Army and the men, women and children of Stalingrad had halted Hitler's army. For the first time, Nazi soldiers were getting a bloody nose. Many a German had died in the battle for Stalingrad, far more than Hitler had expected or the Sixth Army could afford. The German High Command was growing more and more anxious.

***

Days passed... weeks... months. August... September...

By mid-September, much of the city was in German hands. Thousands of old men, women and children were surviving under the rubble, with no food or water. At night, little scavengers emerged from their dens and lairs like foxes hunting for food – rats and mice, birds and their eggs, anything they could catch in their traps and with bare hands. Their nightly bag was hardly enough to feed a sparrow, let alone a whole family. How much longer could they hold out?

Towards the end of September, the Red Army clung on to only a few bridgeheads on the Volga's west bank, none more than a few hundred metres deep. Street after street, square after square, house after house had fallen to the Germans, and the defenders were being pressed back ever closer to the river. The last crossing was constantly under fire, day and night. If reinforcements didn't arrive quickly, all would be lost.

From talking to wounded soldiers Tania knew how desperate the situation was. She was now bumping along in the back of an open-topped lorry with the sniper unit. The convoy was kicking up so much dust that even the river gulls perching on telegraph wires seemed to be wearing dirty grey overcoats. Grazing camels glanced round in alarm, thinking the dust was coming from a prairie fire.

It was a race against time. What if they were too late? General Rodimtsev hurried them along with whoops and whistles, like a cowboy driving on his cattle. Every halt was cut to the minimum. They scarcely had time to brush themselves down and wipe their eyes clean of the grey-brown dust.

The radiator of Tania's truck boiled over – they had no water to fill it up again. But the driver yelled, 'Shut your eyes, girls!'

With a resentful hiss, the bubbling water subsided, the driver did up his trousers and they were off again.

TWENTY-SIX

Even the black crows, ever on the look-out for scraps, had to take evasive action from falling bombs, shells and bullets. The rolling columns were sitting ducks for enemy planes that strafed and bombed them all the way to the Volga. Tania's truck swerved round craters, zig-zagged to avoid being hit, and didn't stop even to help stranded comrades.

Bouncing across the truck wrenched Tania's mind away from the cruel scenes unfolding around her: the wounded in stricken lorries stretching out their arms for help, the scavengers already gnawing at newly-dead flesh.

Their orders were to keep going at all cost. They left it to the ambulance lorries to pick up the dead and dying. Once, they gave way to an ambulance which then took a direct hit intended for them: looking back, Tania saw the crazed face of a young girl engulfed in flames. How Tania wished she was at her gun battery, getting a Messerschmitt in her sights and punching its face with her shiny fists.

As they came closer to the Volga, the dusty dry steppe steadily gave way to green grass and trees. Maples and sturdy limes indicated that they were getting near water. Then came graceful silver birches and weeping willows.

The column passed neat gardens of earth-hugging apple trees, withered tomato and cabbage stalks, golden sunflowers following the sun with smiling faces.

An old woman, strands of grey hair streaming in the breeze, came running towards them. She'd been waiting all day long, hoping to catch a glimpse of her soldier son.

'Take my cucumbers!' she cried. 'They're all I have.'

Tania gazed at her with heavy heart. They could not stop and take her offerings. Hurt showed in the old woman's eyes.

'Look!' she wailed. 'Have some sour cream, apples...'

Her voice trailed away, muffled by the engine's roar. As Tania glanced back, she saw the woman crying, her offerings strewn over the ground, spilt milk seeping into the parched earth.

Now Tania could smell the river – that peculiar swampy, fresh, fishy odour. Ahhh! She had grown up with that smell in her nostrils. It was the very breath of Stalingrad. It was the smell of home.

As they drew close to the city, the soldiers saw a massive, sinister black cloud high in the sky, hovering like a great flock of vultures above the west bank. It was smoke from burning oil dumps.

This was a bad time to be nearing Stalingrad. Even in the twilight, yellow and black hornets filled the sky above the river. Dive bombers were pounding both banks and anything that moved on the still waters.

But the momentum they'd gained strengthened their

determination to get at the enemy. Tania could see it in the excited faces of her comrades, she could feel it in her own fast-beating heart. Although weary, they couldn't wait to throw themselves into battle.

TWENTY-SEVEN

Nothing could have prepared Tania's unit for what confronted them on the bank of the river. They were staring into an inferno. The thunder of thousands of guns blasted their ear-drums until they were fit to burst. Flames, smoke, débris swirled up from the city, making them choke and their eyes smart. Each tied a neckerchief over their mouth and nose to keep out the suffocating smoke.

Tania reeled from the shock. Her first reaction was to flinch, to draw back, to shield her eyes and ears, to sink her steel-helmeted head down into her shoulders. What she was seeing was her home, her school, her Pioneer club being destroyed before her eyes.

Could her mother and the boys be in there somewhere? If so, they stood little chance of coming out alive.

Then her despair turned to anger. What barbarians could wreak such savage devastation on her city?

From their vantage point on Mamayev Kurgan, the Germans had a clear view of the Volga; they could train heavy artillery fire on everything that moved. If that weren't enough, in the gathering twilight the long fingers of their searchlights stretched out, probing the sky, land and river for targets.

Rodimtsev's troops had to get across.

The sniper team was too valuable to be first on the landing boats. That fell to the lot of the Guards who, once across the river, had to jump into the shallows and charge straight up the steep, sandy bank. No one needed to tell them that the longer they dallied, the more likely they were to die.

Tania knew that sooner or later she and her companions would also have to run the gauntlet, in full view of German guns.

She watched helplessly as the river erupted in fierce explosions. Columns of water shot up like cascading fountains, drenching the occupants of the gunboats and civilian craft. As the German gunners adjusted their sights, they scored direct hits on the human cargoes: several boats broke up and sank with barely a survivor.

The river's surface, gleaming with the silver bellies of stunned fish, was also dotted with grey helmets drifting southwards with the current towards the Caspian Sea.

The bright sunshine of late afternoon had faded to a murky dusk which highlighted the huge fires engulfing buildings on the opposite bank and casting grotesque shadows upon the waters.

All at once, Tania felt a hand on her arm. It was Tolya.

'Listen,' he whispered. 'Can you hear that?'

She strained her ears.

'No,' she said.

She could hear the routine sounds of battle: thuds, crashes, rifle fire, screams, as well as the eerie slapping of water against ship bows, the creaking of rowlocks as men rowed hard. But Tolya was hearing something different.

'Wait,' she said. Yes, now she caught the sounds, and she smiled, disbelieving.

Strains of violas and violins, hoarse and trembling, floated solemnly across the Volga, now near, now distant, sometimes muffled by the wind. The music rose above the harsh sounds of battle. It rolled over the waters, over the ruins of the now-silent city, over friend and foe alike, over the tugs and ferry boats, the fishing smacks and barges.

'Do you recognise it?' Tolya asked.

'I think so,' she said, straining her ears. 'It's very familiar. Don't tell me...'

She listened some more.

'Tchaikovsky. It's Tchaikovsky, isn't it?'

'Yes,' he murmured. 'The Sixth Symphony. The Tragic. Third movement. Beautiful.'

They listened together. Goodness knows where the music was coming from. A wind-up gramophone? A wireless on full blast? From the other bank a machine-gun suddenly opened up: *clickety-clack, clickety-clack, clickety-clack*, like a sewing machine. When it stopped, the music welled up even louder.

They listened to the very end. Then a heavy, three-engined bomber flew overhead, a one-note plane, droning away into the distance.

'One of ours,' she said.

'How strange,' he mused.

'What?'

'Oh – the war... the river... the music – all mixed up together, somehow.'

TWENTY-EIGHT

Just then, they noticed a small coracle caught up in the current. Strong eddies from shells and gunboats were spinning the boat round and round. It was like a black water beetle floundering on the water's surface. Besides the man at the oars, the craft held four soldiers. The oarsman was splashing about, desperately trying to regain control. But it was a losing battle.

'Now they'll shoot at it,' said an old soldier casually, tearing off a scrap of newspaper and rolling a cigarette.

A few moments later, a white fountain of water shot up a few metres in front of the little boat's nose.

'Idiots!' the soldier spat out, along with bits of tobacco. He patted down the brown weed in the paper tube, licked the edges and tipped the left-overs into the palm of his hand.

'They should go downstream with the current. Then the Germans would have to change aim all the time. As it is, they're sitting ducks.'

'If they drifted with the current,' came a slow drawl, 'they'd end up either in the Caspian or among the Nazis.'

All eyes were on the little coracle.

More and more fountains flew up and back down again, showering the helpless men. The boat flapped its oars furiously.

'He's a poor shot,' remarked a skinny young sapper. 'Yesterday, they hit one of those boats at third go.'

'No,' someone else said. 'That boat was six times as big. And it was weighed down with equipment and a score of soldiers – it could hardly move.'

Just then, a mortar shell exploded beside the boat, lifting it out of the water. It seemed to dance on the tops of waves, its oars carving thin air. Then it sank back into the river, several metres closer to the far shore.

'Now the machine-gun will bark.'

It was the old soldier's voice again. He drew calmly on his cigarette and blew out a couple of smoke rings.

'As sure as eggs are eggs...'

Right on cue, rows of little jets appeared around the boat, like heavy rain. The spurts of water joined up into a ring. It was incredible that the boat remained afloat.

Silence gripped the onlookers.

Abruptly the oars stopped. Presumably the rower had been killed or badly wounded.

'They'll finish them off now!' muttered a deep bass voice.

Tania was following the fate of the little boat, heart in mouth. All of a sudden – she couldn't help herself – she let out a cheer. One oar began to move, dipping into the river, guiding the boat across the divide. Somehow, miraculously, the little water beetle had reached the middle of the river.

'Another fifty metres and it'll be out of Fritz's sight,' said the sapper to no one in particular.

The mortar started up again. But its roar was drowned by the shouts coming from the opposite shore.

'Go on, lads!'

'You can do it.'

'Only another few metres!'

As though by strength of will, the watchers seemed to have halted the spurts of water. Two or three mortar shells plopped into the water, but the little boat was already out of reach.

'You've done it!' Tania yelled at the top of her voice, tears of joy starting in her eyes. 'You beat them!'

Cheers rang out from the eastern bank. The soldiers resumed their work more energetically, swearing cheerfully.

The old sweat flicked his fag end into the water.

'That's the way we deliver food and ammunition. D'ya see that?' And he stood up and started waving his arms defiantly, shouting encouragement to the soldiers across the river.

TWENTY-NINE

The dark waters continued to flow under a gloomy sky. A cold wind was now blowing from the river. And as soon as the shadows of twilight thickened, the entire bank came to life. The people holding the Volga Crossing scurried about like ants to launch new boatloads of soldiers and supplies. They were the ones on whom the Germans had just poured thousands of mortars and hundreds of bombs for ten days. Earth and sand at the crossing were churned up, as if from a giant plough.

The tall silhouette of an overloaded barge appeared out of the gloom. A towed steamship squawked in a masterly bass. Its siren gave sudden voice to all around it. Lorries revved up their engines. Soldiers grunted and groaned under their heavy burdens – flat boxes of shells, rounds of bullets, grenades and Molotov cocktails. Others were carrying much-needed food for the soldiers and starving civilians – black bread and biscuits, horse-meat salami, sugar and packets of dried eggs.

The barges settled lower and lower in the water.

Meanwhile, the German gunfire didn't let up for a moment. But now, in the dusk, it wasn't as accurate. Enemy spotters couldn't see what was happening on the far bank. Shells were whistling overhead and exploding, momentarily lighting up the haggard trees and cold white sand. Shrapnel was flying all around, ripping into roots and vines in the sandy banks. But no one was paying much attention. The loading continued without a hitch.

'Ready?' A voice startled Tania.

This was it. The snipers filed on to a barge already packed with a few hundred soldiers and supplies – shells, grenades, fuel drums. She found a space next to Tolya amidships, on the port side, where she could look down into the rushing waters. The barge was so low in the river that water flew into her lap as it rocked to and fro.

Tania's mind was in turmoil. She was going home – but like a rabbit returning to its warren, knowing that a pack of hungry foxes lay in wait.

To reach Stalingrad, they had to run the gauntlet of enemy fire. One direct hit on the fuel and ammo supplies and all the soldiers – or pieces of them – would be floating in the river. She shuddered at the thought, knowing the odds were stacked against them. All they could do was hope.

'Full speed ahead!' yelled the captain.

Off they went. The stretch of foaming water between barge and bank began to widen; waves splashed over the sides, and hundreds of pairs of eyes looked with alarm to the western bank where the burning city was covered in greyish-black smoke.

'Dive bombers!' someone shouted.

About fifty metres from their barge, a tall white column with foaming crown suddenly shot out of the water, then cascaded back, splashing them with spray.

Straight away, a second column, even closer, spurted up; then a third. Splinters and shrapnel rained down on deck. Wounded men cried out, first sharp screams, then confused groans.

An arm grabbed Tania's neck, clinging on for grim death. So strong was the grip, she thought it might be a German trying to strangle her. But in an explosive flash she saw who it was – Lena! The poor girl was petrified. Her face was contorted into a horrified mask, her whole body trembled uncontrollably. She buried her face in Tania's shoulder.

'Now, now, Lena, be brave. We'll soon be there.'

Like a dam bursting, the tears flooded down Lena's cheeks and Tania's neck.

'That's it, that's it, get it out.'

As Lena's tears subsided into gentle sobs, they both looked round in alarm. A heavy shell had hit the deck. Flames shot up and dark smoke covered the whole barge, accompanied by a long, drawn-out human cry. Clinging desperately to the side, Tania saw shattered timber struts and planks floating on the water and, amidst the débris, a score of helmets.

The barge was sinking fast.

THIRTY

The shell had sliced through the flat wooden deck, landed in the engine room and exploded, leaving a gaping hole in the starboard side just below the water line.

More terrifying than the groans of the wounded caught in the blast, more terrifying than the heavy clatter of pounding boots, more terrifying than the cry 'We're drowning!' echoing across the river... was the sound of water gushing and gurgling into the barge.

The explosion had come in midstream – too far out to reach safety on the east bank, too close to the west bank to escape German bullets. Already the weight of water was dragging the ship down, tipping it to starboard and washing waves over the side.

Had Tania come so close to her city, only to drown within sight of the streets she knew so well? The water covered her ankles and was creeping higher and higher.

Her gloomy thoughts were suddenly diverted to a dark form lying at her feet. Rivulets were running to and fro across the face, and there was a trickle of bubbles at the mouth.

She recognised the bushy eyebrows.

Tolya!

She grabbed his head and pulled it up to her knees. He was a dead weight – but slight shivers through his wet shirt told her he was still alive.

She couldn't do much on her own. To one side of her was Lena, her face buried in her hands.

'Lena!' Tania cried sharply. 'Snap out of it and give me a hand. Tolya's wounded.'

Lena squinted through her fingers. 'Where's he hurt?'

'Never mind! Take one arm, I'll take the other. Let's get the river out of his lungs. Come on, move.'

Her bullying worked. Lena immediately forgot her own misery and helped pull the still figure on to the bench, turning him over on his stomach and pumping his arms. He must have swallowed half the river, for water gushed out as if from a village pump, slowly dying to a trickle. The last dribbles were accompanied by a deep moaning that came up from his boots. Tolya was back among the living.

'Where does it hurt?' Tania shouted over the hubbub.

'M-my head,' he murmured.

She swiftly passed her fingers through his hair, over his neck and face, finding plenty of bumps, but no cuts or signs of blood.

'S-some-thing hit me, and I-I passed out.'

'You seem to be in one piece,' she said. Then: 'Can you swim?'

Tolya nodded slowly. Lena shook her head.

'Lena, keep between us; we'll try to grab a plank or something and make for the shore.'

THIRTY-ONE

All at once, above the guns, screams, shouts, gurgles, came a bull-like roar. It came from a tall soldier, a man with three stripes. He was shouting orders and tearing off his greatcoat. Tania had noticed him on the bank, pacing up and down impatiently, an upright figure, serious and stern, with a farmer's weather-beaten face and heavy hands. His thin, unsmiling lips, bright black eyes like a crow's, and dark, greying hair spoke of a man you wouldn't want to meddle with, yet one you'd trust with your life.

The sergeant was removing his coat and rolling it into a bundle.

'Someone, hold my ankles,' he bawled. 'I'll plug the hole with my greatcoat.'

Tania glanced round. No one moved.

'Come on, Lena,' she yelled. 'Quick!'

The sergeant was already half over the side, head first into the river, when they grabbed his ankles and clung on for grim death.

The pressure of water threw him against the splintered wood of the barge; they heard a sickening thud as his head hit the side. Tania's first thought was that he'd been knocked out. It was as if the Volga's mighty spirit, the *vodyanoi*, was trying to tear away this obstruction and force its way into the hole.

Minutes dragged by. Others began helping to hold his legs, and sailors inside the barge were frantically patching up the torn hole. By the time many hands had hauled him up and laid him on deck his eyes were shut, his brow was streaming dark red blood, and green river bile was dribbling from his purple lips. He lay there motionless.

Tania the nurse took over. His life lay in her hands.

'Move back. Give him air!' she shouted.

She bent over his head, wiped away the bile and cleared the air passages to his nose and mouth, pumping his chest and blowing hard into his mouth – all the things she'd learned in first aid. Though she knew it made no difference to the man, she wiped clean his unshaven cheeks and bandaged his forehead with a towel someone passed her.

In vain. Tania gazed sadly at the deathly pallor of his face.

All at once his chest heaved, the floodgates opened and the river spilled from his nose and mouth on to the deck. A few minutes later he opened his eyes.

Tania smiled with relief. She'd done it! Her mum would be proud.

The hero's face was calm, his black eyes stared at the anxious faces bending over him. He coughed and gasped for air, clearing his windpipe. Then he said hoarsely, 'Right, let's get on with it.'

Thanks to that one man, four hundred soldiers reached Stalingrad's west bank.

So too did the sniper team. They owed their lives to him – and he owed his to Tania.

Now the snipers could go into action. Their turn had come.

THIRTY-TWO

As the listing barge came closer to the bank, the German fire intensified. The barge was too close to enemy positions for the Germans to drop bombs or fire shells. But that didn't stop machine-gunners sweeping the deck, back and forth, killing anyone unlucky enough to be in the way.

The survivors lay flat on the deck, shielded by the bows tilted by the weight of water in the stern. Tania held her breath, listening to the deadly *rat-tat-tat* followed by plops and splashes as bullets harmlessly hit the water, by *ping-pings* as they ricocheted across the wooden deck and sides, by soft thuds and shrieks as they found a target.

So close were the enemy gunners, that their gutteral taunts could plainly be heard:

'Hey, Russky! *Bool-bool! Bool-bool!*'

'*Bool-bool*' was the sound of Russians drowning.

***

The barge was almost there. The captain was making for a jetty sheltered from enemy guns by a bend in the river. It was an oasis still held by men fighting for the Red October munitions plant

As they drew closer to the shore, Tania gazed through

the gloom at the plant lit up by flares – at the foundry's towering hulk, the wet glistening rails touched with rust, the steel girders scattered about the cavernous cathedral of a workshop, the piles of coal and coke, slag and clinker.

Lieutenant Zaitsev gathered his sniper flock about him, running his eye over them to make sure they were unharmed.

'Follow me!' he shouted. 'Close ranks.'

He clambered on to the jetty, with the unit following. Tolya, still groggy, needed Lena and Tania to give him a helping hand, while Salami carried his rifle and a box of hand grenades.

As they entered the factory loading bay, Tania stared around. Everywhere there were shell holes and craters where men were now living, peering out now and then for a glimpse of the enemy. They kept one step ahead of the Germans, diving into each new crater even before the dust had settled and hoping it wouldn't be bombed twice.

'We'll hole up here,' said Zaitsev, as they all tumbled into a workshop basement, 'and wait for further orders.'

They settled down to an early morning breakfast of black bread, raw onion and salami.

The factory yards were empty. The wind whistled through shattered windows and broken doors. Over the next few days Tania watched sadly as the last of the smoke-stacks toppled. On the first day there had been six, the next day three, then two, and, today, only one was left standing, full of shell holes and with the top knocked off.

Yet, miraculously, it stood firm, as if to spite its attackers.

Every night the battle for Red October marked a new page in the war. No longer were the Germans hurling shells into the sky over a great distance. This was now a battle of hammer-blows, straight and fast: from stone wall to stone wall, bunker to bunker, room to room.

The sun rose over the newly-dug craters whose depths its light never reached, perhaps afraid of uncovering what lay there. It shone through holes in the remaining chimney before lighting up sliced and twisted metal cisterns and dozens of freight wagons huddled together. It lit up the mounds of dead bodies beside the ruins of factory workshops, friend and foe sometimes sleeping in each other's dead embrace.

***

On the fourth morning, the sniper team was pitched into battle. There was no time for them to be briefed on where best to set up a sniper's nest. They were despatched to the ground floor of what had once been a repair shop.

As they took up positions beside the broken windows, Zaitsev put a finger to his lips, signalling the band to gather round.

'I thought I heard a noise upstairs. No idea if it's ours or theirs.'

Just then, they heard a clatter of boots overhead: they were not alone.

'Wait here.'

Zaitsev crept up the stone steps leading to the upper floor, pistol in hand, and disappeared round a dark bend. It was several minutes before he returned.

'Germans,' he hissed. 'Nine or ten, as far as I can make out.'

'How are we going to flush them out?' asked Salami.

'Patience,' said Zaitsev calmly. 'They must know we're down here, and that they're trapped; the only way out is to get past us.'

That night the unit rested four at a time, while the others stood guard at the windows, doors and stairwell.

Upstairs, the Germans made no sound.

THIRTY-THREE

This was Tania's first real action. During her rest period, she didn't relax for a moment. She was tense and scared as she trained her rifle on the stairs. She could see Lena trembling, her eyes large with fear. Tania did her best to calm her – which helped take her own mind off worrying.

'I bet those Fritzes are terrified out of their wits, knowing we're down here.'

'I'm scared,' Lena muttered.

'Everyone is.'

'Really?'

'Of course – even Vasily Ivanovich.' Tania stared at the chief, who looked as cool as a cucumber.

'Don't let appearances fool you,' said Tania. 'Underneath, his heart's going nineteen to the dozen and his knees are like jelly. But he doesn't let it show.'

Lena thought for a moment, then set to checking her rifle and sights, apparently reassured.

'When d'you think Fritz will make a move?'

'When it gets light, I guess.'

Sure enough, when morning came, dead on six, a footfall at the top of the stairs had them all primed for action. What they didn't expect were two long-fused satchel bombs to come hurtling towards them.

No one moved. Tania was paralysed with fear.

It was Tolya's quick thinking that saved them. Quick as a flash he darted forward, picked up the bombs, ran up the shaky steps and hurled them into the room above. The surprised Germans had no time to return the compliment. The charges exploded, clearly wounding some, judging by their screams of pain.

Tania grinned with relief.

'Well done!' said Zaitsev to Tolya. 'You saved our lives.'

To the rest, he said quietly, 'That was quick thinking – the mark of a first-class sniper. What can we learn from this?' Answering his own question, he continued: 'Number One: they've no grenades – otherwise they'd have thrown them at us. Number Two: they'll need medical assistance if they want to treat the wounded. Prepare for action.'

Again, a tense wait. Beads of sweat broke out on Tania's brow. But action wasn't long in coming. A soldier appeared at the top of the steps, waving a dirty white handkerchief. Behind him came two men holding up a wounded soldier.

Beckoning the Germans to halt, Zaitsev waved a hand at his unit to take cover. It was lucky he did. The wounded man suddenly dropped to the ground, revealing a soldier with a tommy-gun crouching behind him. The man fired two bursts, spraying the workshop walls with bullets; one burst went right between Zaitsev's legs.

Tania was too stunned to react. What if the bullets

had struck Zaitsev? Who would take over? It taught her a lesson: don't think, act! Like Zaitsev.

Before the German could fire a third burst, Zaitsev raised his pistol and shot him dead, while the German's companions fled back upstairs.

The stalemate continued: the Germans couldn't come down for fear of being shot; the snipers couldn't go up for the same reason. Twenty-four hours passed. At last, Tolya whispered, 'Why don't a couple of us cross over into the workshop opposite and track the Germans through the windows? We should be able to pick them off with a telescopic rifle.'

Zaitsev agreed. But who would do it? It needed a crack shot. All eyes were on Vasily Ivanovich.

'I'd go myself,' he muttered, 'but someone has to take charge here in case they make a break for it. Tolya, Tania. You got top scores on the rifle range. See to it.'

A baptism of fire. Tania didn't know about Tolya, but she had mixed feelings – a thrill of excitement and a frisson of fear. Not fear for her life, exactly, but another fear. She would have to kill, whether she liked it or not. No time to sit down with Tolya and talk it over. They were under orders. Don't think, act!

Together they left the workshop by a side door, keeping close to the shadows and edging along the pock-marked wall – so that the Germans above didn't spot them. At one point, the space between workshops was littered with débris – piles of steel girders, rusting rails, red clinker and several craters. If they made a dash for it, from one cover to the next, they might succeed in crossing without being seen.

A siren suddenly wailed from one of the nearby plants, making them both jump. Almost at once the dark, ruined walls were lit by pink and white gun-flashes.

'Let's go!' whispered Tolya.

THIRTY-FOUR

In no time at all they were dashing through the half-open door of a derelict building. They entered cautiously and climbed up the shattered stairwell to the floor above. The only sign of life was a large grey cat sitting in one corner scowling, a half-eaten rat at her feet.

Taking up their posts at two windows some twenty metres apart, they had a good view of the Germans. As far as Tania could see, there were seven still alive. They were nervously smoking and chatting, heedless of watching eyes. One was trying to operate a walkie-talkie, no doubt attempting to summon help. It seemed unreal. If the enemy had been in trenches, poking their guns over the top and firing, it would have been natural to return fire. But here they were sitting quietly, asking for it. Tania felt like shouting out a warning. Of course, she didn't. It's them or us, she said to herself.

'Tania!' hissed Tolya. 'Take out the radio operator first, then the pair closest to you. I'll look after the four opposite me. OK? After five.

'One... two... three... four... FIVE!'

She had the man clearly in her sights. She'd done this a hundred times before on the rifle range. She aimed to hit him squarely between the eyes. Yet... she hesitated, her finger stuck on the trigger. Her German reminded her of a boy at school: same fair hair parted down the middle, same ruddy cheeks, light down on his top lip – a feeble excuse for a moustache. His long fingers were tapping urgently on his transmitter – hands as fine as those of a concert pianist.

Only after the jolt of Tolya's exploding shot did she spring to life.

Her operator vanished backwards over the wooden box he'd been sitting on.

Her first kill!

They didn't have time to compare notes. The Germans were in a panic, unable to work out the direction of fire. At first they seemed to think it came from the stairs. That gave the two snipers a second opportunity to line up their victims.

Simultaneously, two more shots rang out, one from Tolya, one from Tania... and two more men fell from sight. What spoiled it was the blood-curdling scream and cry 'Mama!' from the man she'd shot. The cigarette he'd been smoking stayed stuck to his bottom lip.

Four down, three to go.

Tania could see the survivors on their hands and knees, gesticulating wildly towards an invisible enemy. But their gestures all indicated different directions. They were panic-stricken.

Tolya fired another shot and brought on another scream.

Two to go. They divided them up.

She could see her German cowering in a corner,

his hands in front of him in prayer. She could hear his cries, though she couldn't understand what he was saying – probably 'Please don't shoot me...'

The bullet must have gone through the man's hands, for he pitched forward, arms outstretched, blood spurting from his face and hands.

Tolya fired at the same time. Then he slowly stood up. As she looked towards him, she was astonished to see his shoulders shaking and his hands over his eyes. He was crying softly.

Tania herself was close to tears.

'I suppose it's natural,' she said in a wobbly voice. 'You know, first time. It must get easier, huh? We get hardened to it, like doctors at their first sight of blood – don't you think?'

Tolya was silent. He turned away, ashamed. She waited for him to pick up his rifle and make a move towards the stairwell.

'Let's get back,' he said hoarsely. Then, as an afterthought, he added quietly, 'Don't let on.'

'Of course not.'

Then Tania did something strange. She stood on tiptoe and kissed Tolya's moist cheeks.

'Mission accomplished,' she said. She blushed as she spoke. This was the second time she'd dared kiss him. It seemed so natural: to give him courage. Truth to tell, there was more, though she would hardly admit it. She was drawn to this shy, quiet boy with the moist brown eyes and soft sandy hair on his cheeks and chin.

Her heart beat fast as she hurried along beside him. At the same time, she desperately tried to banish her feelings. After all, this was war.

When they'd rejoined the unit, Zaitsev led the way up the dark steps. Outside the upstairs door, he paused. They all breathed heavily as he counted slowly up to ten.

Then he burst in.

Seven Germans lay on the floor dead. Two other bodies were lying in the far corner, covered with sacking.

Tania couldn't look.

After this burst of activity, the snipers were disappointed to have to kick their heels for several days, awaiting further orders. There was plenty of time to talk about Tania's and Tolya's bravery. Yet both were reluctant to talk about it. Tania had never understood why her grandfather refused to talk about his adventures back in the Great War. Now, for the first time, she understood.

Killing is something you don't want to think, let alone talk about.

THIRTY-FIVE

Apart from all the soldiers, you would have thought the city was deserted. No sign of human life. No laughter. No chatter. No babies crying. But if you put your ear to the ground, you might just have caught a sigh or whisper or groan. This was the underground people.

In a courtyard close to the sniper position there had once been a pretty little cottage. A direct hit had blown it sky-high, leaving nothing but rubble. The husband had been killed, leaving a widow and three children who had sheltered in the cellar. And there they remained, to sit out the war. The widow had taken her pots, pickled cabbage and apples, dried mushrooms and tomatoes, even the nanny goat – though it gave no milk because it was kept in the dark. In one corner was a little stove on top of a rain-barrel.

Now and then they came up for air. Between the collapsed cottage walls was a trap-door made of old floorboards, with a dozen steps leading down. Two little girls, one ten, the other eight, blinked their big curious eyes in the moonlight. Living in the underworld, it was easy to lose track of time. A flash from an exploding shell momentarily lit up the jagged battlements of what had once been a department store. The air reeked of burning rubber, wood, tarpaulin and death.

The family had been due to leave on a paddle steamer that never came. German guns had sent it to the river-bed with a full cargo of women and children. Only three women had managed to swim to a sandbank; all the children drowned.

So the widow stayed put. She told her children, 'We've enough food to last a month or so – until we drive the Germans out. And if a bomb falls on us – poof! – that's fate. We'll all go together...' She crossed herself and shrugged.

Not far away, groans were coming from beneath a sheet of corrugated iron. A thin ray of moonlight filtered through the shutters of a basement window, touched the boots of a wounded soldier, played on a metal button of his greatcoat, climbed up to a table and a dull silver samovar.

The smell was unmistakable: decay, rotting flesh, gangrene. The basement was full of about twenty wounded soldiers. They were nursed by a young woman, Zina. Before the war she'd been a medical student, halfway through her studies. Now, each night, she crawled out under heavy fire to reach the wounded and carry them on her back to safety.

The only field hospitals were across the river. At first she carried or dragged casualties all the way to the Volga's edge, waited patiently for an empty supply boat, staying with them on the eastern bank. She soon realised there was no point: she'd seen thousands of wounded dumped on the sand, as far as the eye could see, calling for water, screaming or crying, some without arms or legs.

Even if they'd managed to make the six kilometres to Balashchov Hospital, there were no beds and little equipment. So Zina set up her underground refuge, giving some wounded soldiers hope, some their last days in peace and care, some the dignity of death.

Often there was no food and water. The city had been without fresh water since the August raids destroyed the pumping station. Sometimes Zina would make a hole in a drainpipe or melt icicles. There was a brave Tatar cook who used to fill a large thermos with tea or soup; he'd fasten it to his back and crawl out to Zina under fire. On one occasion, bullets hit the thermos and soaked him to the skin in hot soup.

As for medical supplies, whenever Zina could, she tried to find clean bandages and medicines. At the same time, she tried to bring back some cabbage heads and frozen bread or potatoes. It was tough going – especially after giving blood every week. But if she didn't give blood, her soldiers would die.

Steps amid the rubble led down to a rabbit warren of corridors and vaults; every nook and cranny was filled to overflowing with elderly men and women, mothers and little children, their eyes filled with fear: that someone might steal their space or their hard-earned scraps.

They were all filthy, lice-ridden, starving,. They picked clean the bones of dead horses. Mice and rat meat was a luxury. Some raided army rubbish bins for rotten potato peel, poked around in derelict houses, even sneaked through the army lines to find ears of wheat to boil.

If anyone had been walking across a bombed site near Zina's 'hospital', they might have heard an odd sound, muffled, distant. It was a noise as out of place as a nightingale's song in the depths of winter.

The music was coming from the end of a long tunnel which opened out into a spacious basement. The roof had fallen in and, on top of a pile of broken stones and timber, tilted to one side, stood... a grand piano!

At the piano, on a wooden crate, sat an elderly man with a gaunt face and sunken cheeks. He was wearing concert dress: black trousers and jacket, white shirt with winged collar and black bow tie. All about him, sitting on the floor, were over a hundred people.

At the end of the piece, he turned to the audience and announced in a deep voice, 'Johann Sebastian Bach. Siciliano.' Then he added softly, 'If there are any police present, I hope you won't shoot me for breaking the ban on German composers.'

The pianist played as if he were in a Moscow concert hall, swept up on a wave of musical passion. When he finished, his head flung back, arms at his sides, a hushed silence hung over the audience.

Then, all at once, clapping could be heard coming from the other side of the far wall. A German voice shouted, 'Play, Meister, more Bach, *bitte*.'

The pianist stretched his fingers, smiled and murmured, 'Bach. Prelude and Fugue in C Major.'

War is full of surprises. Both sides do their best to kill

each other. If the pianist had popped his head above ground, that same German would not have thought twice about shooting him. Yet, for a brief moment, they could forget war and enjoy music together. War hardens the heart, music softens it.

THIRTY-SIX

Two unexpected guests turned up at the sniper snug. Tania recognised one of them at once. She was pleased to see the brush-haired figure of General Rodimtsev again. Despite constant air raids, he insisted on visiting all his troops and boosting morale.

The other officer had dark, wavy hair, wide black eyebrows, a potato nose, thick lips and a deeply-wrinkled face. You would have taken him for a typical Russian peasant. His expression was rather like that of a bad-tempered pug-dog who'd found a cat in his kennel. Judging by the stars on his lapel, he was someone to be reckoned with.

Rodimtsev introduced him.

'Comrade snipers, let me present General Chuikov, Commander of the 62nd Army.'

So this was Chuikov! He was well-known for his explosive temper. A short man with broad shoulders, he edged round the makeshift crate-table to take a closer look at the snipers. His scowl made it clear he didn't like what he saw. Was it their age, or the presence of girls?

All at once, he stopped before Zaitsev and snapped, 'How do you see your mission?'

Zaitsev had a stock answer ready. 'To kill as many Germans as possible.'

Turning to his team, Zaitsev added his usual 'Right?'

'Right, Vasily Ivanovich,' they chorused.

'Idiots!' yelled Chuikov. 'Every soldier wants to kill as many enemy as he can. Your mission is different. It's not how many, it's who. Got it? Your job is to shoot officers, the more senior the better, so that we force them to keep changing command. We wear them down – got it?'

These last words were addressed to Zaitsev.

'Yes, Comrade General!'

Zaitsev's words said one thing, his eyes said another. Clearly, he resented being shamed in front of his unit.

As the two generals turned to go, Rodimtsev abruptly halted and, to Tania's embarrassment, called her over.

'Tanechka,' he said familiarly.

Here it comes, was her first thought. He's had second thoughts about girls in the firing line: he now thinks a woman's duty is to patch up the wounded, swab up the blood, comfort the dying.

But she was wrong. Rodimtsev's kindly face smiled awkwardly.

'How's it going?'

'Fine, Comrade General. Glad to serve.'

A frown flitted across his face.

'Drop the bullshit. You're not a natural killer, are you?'

She had to be frank.

'Well, no-o-o, it doesn't come easy.'

'You and Chekhov did a fine job. I'm pleased. But that was kill or be killed. Are you tough enough to kill in cold blood?'

He could see a shadow of doubt in her eyes.

'Look, I don't want you sitting here, twiddling your thumbs until we need you. I've arranged for you and Chekhov to meet the enemy face to face. Know your enemy! That's the secret of successful warfare.'

What on earth was he driving at? Were they to put on German uniform and go behind the lines?

'I want you and Chekhov to report tomorrow afternoon to Captain Dyatlenko at the Intelligence Centre. You'll be escorting a batch of prisoners across the Volga. Good luck.'

He swivelled on his heel and was gone, leaving her stunned.

Tolya was just as confused as Tania. But it seemed that Zaitsev had provided reports on each of his snipers to Rodimtsev. And he'd evidently picked out those who needed toughening up.

Next afternoon, the pair took their rifles and dressed warmly in white snow-suits. Winter was in the air. These were the first days of November; only a dusting of snow had fallen, but the snowless wind whistling through the ruins was icy cold.

The Volga's waters were chained and heavy. Today, tomorrow or very soon the first skin of ice would cover the river – and that would make crossings almost impossible.

THIRTY-SEVEN

The once-grand building with its yellow stucco walls on the main street had taken a battering since Tania's encounter with Major-General Rogatin. A side wall and part of the roof had caved in and a bitterly cold, gusty wind was howling through the gaps.

Tania and Tolya showed their papers, explaining their appointment with Captain Dyatlenko. The sentry summoned a uniformed female orderly who silently led the way down some stairs. Tania was surprised to discover that the former Secret Police headquarters was almost as deep as it was high. The basement consisted of four floors housing prison cells, stores, interrogation and torture rooms.

The orderly led them down a long corridor dimly lit by oil lamps, and smelling of boiled cabbage. Its whitewashed walls and flagstone floors reminded Tania of the hospital where they'd left poor Nina. But there were no wards here, no white-coated nurses and doctors, just row upon row of barred cells behind which dirty, unshaven men stood in ragged, olive-green greatcoats, staring sullenly, miserably into space.

The office to which they were taken was cold and cramped. It was more like the archives of a vast library, with cardboard boxes of files lining the walls and standing on the floor in tall piles.

The officer at the desk gave them a nervous smile.

'I'm Captain N.D. Dyatlenko, Chief Interrogator,' he said, fidgeting with papers on his desk. 'I've been expecting you – you're to be our prisoner-of-war escort.'

As they introduced themselves, he kept repeating their words and muttered in German, '*Gut. Ach so. Bestimmt.*'

Perhaps that's what living underground does to you, Tania thought.

'What do you think of the prisoners?' he suddenly asked.

It was Tolya who answered.

'I feel more pity than hatred, to be honest.'

'Really?' He seemed shocked. 'Don't be fooled by appearances. They sang a different song before, when they were murdering every Russian they could get their hands on, when they were burning down villages and overrunning our towns.'

He wiped the saliva from his lips and stood up.

'Come. Let me show you our Trophy Room.'

He took them down to the bottom floor and unlocked a large, stuffy storeroom.

'We search all prisoners upon arrival. You'd be surprised what they keep in their knapsacks.'

Tania gazed curiously at the belongings piled high in the storeroom. Gradually her curiosity turned to disbelief.

There were old women's brown shawls and grey knitted scarves, skirts and coarse linen underwear, scores of pairs of woollen stockings, embroidered blouses and coloured jumpers, children's shoes, even nappies.

'Why?' she gasped. 'What are they for?'

'Mostly trophies,' he said dryly. 'To show to the folks back home: "Hey, Mutti, see what Russian peasants wear!" And to show to his mates – having a good laugh at a pair of drawers ripped off an old woman. One soldier collected twenty-two pairs of thick stockings; another had four pairs of women's felt boots. Hardly goods to sell – wouldn't you agree?'

Tania moved around the room, astounded at the heaps of clothing, footwear, even cheap jewellery – rings, necklaces, little crosses, earrings, bracelets.

In one corner was a sack full of children's toys: carved wooden bears, a cockerel and a fox on a see-saw, several dolls and a little soldier in a red star cap.

'What you don't see,' Dyatlenko muttered, 'are the cows and sheep, the poultry and grain they took. You don't see the villages they stripped bare, leaving people to starve. You don't see the villagers they flogged and tortured till they gave up their last bowl of grain, or the homes they burned down, sometimes with whole families inside, or the young women they marched off to Germany, leaving the old and young to starve or freeze to death.'

Tolya had halted in front of a cardboard box, and was looking puzzled.

'Best come away,' the officer said sharply.

'Why? What's this? Looks like…' He stopped in

mid-sentence, his hand stifling a cry.

The box was full to overflowing with hair of every type – grey and chestnut, snow-white and jet-black, blonde and ginger; wavy, straight, tangled, even pigtails with little faded ribbons still on them.

'I don't believe it! Why?'

'Who knows?' the officer replied slowly. 'To humiliate their victims? To stuff cushions with? To take home as war trophies? Now, do you still pity them?'

They both stood rooted to the spot, unable to speak.

After a few moments, Tania said quietly, 'I feel sick.'

Later, back in his office, Captain Dyatlenko said, 'Go and get a good night's sleep. There's a room ready for you, fairly basic, but clean enough. You'll be called early tomorrow morning.'

They were glad to shut the door of their room. It was no more than a cell used for special prisoners, with a bunk on either side. But they were relieved to be left alone with their thoughts after what they had just seen. They ate little of the meal brought in. Neither wanted to talk.

After a tepid wash, shared with scuttling brown and silver cockroaches, Tania took off her boots and lay down on the bunk.

She was soon floating in and out of sleep. While her body rested, her mind whirred and chimed like an old clock. What sort of person could cut off women's hair? Burn families alive? Flog peasants for their last bowl of grain? She couldn't understand it. Were Germans human? They were worse than wild beasts.

Who had taught them to be so cruel? When they were murdering little children, didn't they think of their own brothers and sisters?

In her mind's eye she saw the fair-haired German she'd shot. Perhaps he deserved it, after all.

THIRTY-EIGHT

Tania woke up in a sweat. Her first instinct was to touch her hair. Yes, it was still there, damp with perspiration. She sat up in bed, unplaiting and re-plaiting her hair, smoothing it down with one hand. In the darkness she couldn't see the time. Just at that moment, a knock and a voice at the door made her jump.

'Be prepared!'

'Always prepared!' she answered, automatically using the Young Pioneers' motto.

Switching on the bare bulb, she shook Tolya and told him, 'You snore.'

'So do you.'

'Nonsense,' Tania retorted as she took first turn at the wash-basin. She stank of sweat. Her hair was a mess, tangled and greasy, and she itched all over from flea-bites. How she longed for a good soaking. But the water was freezing cold and rusty brown. A little pile of salt had been left on the dirty mirror shelf: she rubbed her teeth with it.

'After you in the bath-house,' called Tolya. 'You girls take all day.'

Tolya had finished his ablutions even before Tania had tied her laces. Off they went for breakfast in the guard room, stopping at the communal lavatory on their way.

They helped themselves to a plate of cold porridge, a glass of cold, weak tea and half a slice of black bread which bounced off the table like a wooden spoon. They chewed and drank in silence, as did the four guards across the table.

At seven, they were outside Captain Dyatlenko's office.

'Right – Corporal Chekhov, did you sleep well?'

'Not really,' Tolya said.

'And you, Comrade Belova?'

'Between flea-bites, I had nightmares,' Tania replied.

The captain shrugged. Then, clearing his throat, he asked, 'Can you handle a pistol?'

'Yes,' Tolya replied. 'We were taught to handle guns at sniper school, and we killed Germans with rifles. But neither of us has fired a pistol in battle.'

'Let's hope you never have to. Sign here for the guns. Just in case, eh?'

'How many prisoners must we sign for?' Tania asked.

Captain Dyatlenko gave a humourless laugh.

'You'll have two hundred, give or take a few losses on the crossing. No point in signing for them; no one's going to count them at the bottom of the river or on the other side. You'll have two guards with you; they've already taken the prisoners down to the river.

'You're on the steamship *Swallow*. Our poor swallow's had its wings clipped: it took ten direct hits in a single crossing yesterday, though the crew have done their best to patch her up in the night. The old tub should make it across on tow. Good luck.'

We'll need it, by the sound of things, Tania thought to herself. Other thoughts came into her mind. Why risk their lives taking scum across the Volga, when they could be killing Germans? What if a shell blew them sky-high? Never mind prisoners-of-war, what about them? They were the Red Army's secret weapon – General Rodimtsev had said so himself.

Even down in the bowels of the earth, they could hear and feel the early morning bombardment; it had begun on the stroke of seven.

They made their way down to the jetty. It was bitterly cold. Gone were the brief days of autumn when fish would rise and spread great circles over the river's mirror-like surface, and late cranes would fly croaking overhead. Now a strong north-easterly was blowing and dark, wet clouds were rising in the sky. The mist was beginning to freeze and leave a white powder upon the trees on the embankment.

Puddles left in shell craters were covered by white sheets of thin ice. The earth rang like glass to the sound of boots and in the west, above the stone lace of the dead city, a red sunrise was heralding the new day.

As they reached the river, they were exposed to the wind – so cold and relentless, it made the waters crackle. The river's surface was covered by a rippling, slender icy crust. Small ice floes, murmuring, clashing, crumbling, climbing on top of each other, were floating down the Volga.

On one ice floe, Tania shuddered to see an ugly black crow pecking at something. She drew Tolya's attention to it.

'Yes,' he said, 'yesterday I heard that a passing steamer had picked up the remains of a sailor in a blue and white striped vest; he'd stuck fast to the ice.'

Tania shivered, hoping that they wouldn't end up as crow meat.

Looking up and down the river, she noticed that when the oarsmen dipped their blades into the water, little slivers of ice clung to them, like sugar to a spoon. The wind was snatching up the black smoke from steamship funnels, spreading it over the river and tearing it to pieces on floes that reared up in a giant quiff. The blunt-nosed prows of barges slowly forced their way through dark waters which immediately turned to ice at the stern.

Never before had Tania seen boats working so late in the season.

On board *Swallow*, the captain, with a long grey moustache like a Cossack and a face brick-red from the wind, joked, 'Our first Polar navigation.'

A barge, creaking under its heavy load, was approaching the west bank, bringing tanks, horses, ammunition, bread, under fire from above and ahead, braving the icy crossing to give a lifeline to the Stalingrad defenders.

The prison ship could scarcely be classed as life-saving cargo. But what else could they do with prisoners? Dump them in the Volga? Tania stared at them with no pity in her heart. Here she was, sixteen years old, responsible for the fate of two hundred Germans! After what she'd seen in the Trophy Room, she was tempted to shoot the lot of them…

The prisoners were standing, huddled together on deck, some with ragged blankets round their shoulders and string or wire in place of belts. They were stamping their feet and blowing on their frozen fingers.

'It's a long way to come to see the Volga!' muttered the Captain. And he gave a scornful laugh.

THIRTY-NINE

The Germans stared miserably at the crackling ice. No doubt some were wondering whether their own planes would send them to a watery grave in this godforsaken land.

Fountains of water spurted up from the waves, fizzing and gurgling like a samovar. Bombers danced in and out of searchlights. It was hard to tell whose bombers, whose searchlights.

But, by a miracle, they made it safely to the other side.

On the eastern bank, another few thousand prisoners were waiting, guarded by no more than a dozen or so soldiers. Once the last contingent had joined, they marched off trying to keep in step, billy cans jangling at their waists.

Tania watched them go, wondering where they were heading. All the way to Siberia? Would they ever see their homes and families again? No doubt they were thinking the same thoughts. The straggly line of Germans followed the twists and turns of the road like some dark, meandering stream. Their only consolation was that every step took them out of range of bombs and shells.

Tania couldn't care less. She had done her job. Now all she and Tolya had to do was return to Stalingrad.

The steamship, meanwhile, was being loaded with

more supplies. As they stood waiting for its return journey, a voice shouted out, 'Hey, you two!'

It was a young lieutenant.

'I need someone to guard supplies.' He pointed a finger at Tolya. 'You'll do, lad. You're armed.'

There was no point in arguing with an officer.

'Perhaps it's just as well,' sighed Tolya. 'If we split up, there's more chance of one of us making it back to base. Silly to risk us both.' He was right. They'd done their job. No sense chancing the trip together.

'All right,' she said. 'I'll hitch a lift on one of the barges. I don't fancy hanging about here for this old tub.'

As they parted, she reflected on Rodimtsev's wisdom. She and Tolya had both been tempered by their brush with the enemy. After what they'd been through, they'd have no more qualms about killing Germans.

She wandered along the jetty to a barge being loaded up with newly-arrived soldiers. You could see from the awkward way they carried their weapons that they hadn't yet seen action.

Most of them were slant-eyed, dark-haired, squat men from Siberia – a merry bunch whose good humour was exaggerated by nervous tension. They were preparing themselves by guzzling their vodka ration.

Their commanding officer grudgingly let Tania on board.

'Hey, girl, come and have a swig!' a soldier shouted cheerily, waving a bottle above his head.

'Come and sit on my lap, little pigeon!' yelled another.

Tania tossed her head disdainfully and found space in the prow, sitting with her knees pressed against her chest for the ride.

The boat was halfway across, when the sky suddenly filled with fiery red and orange balls which rained down on the river. The barge was bucking and twisting through water spouts that reared up out of the water.

Another fifty metres and they'd be safe.

'What's it like over there?' asked someone slightly older than her father. His question was more to divert attention than to seek an answer.

'Tough,' she said.

His companion, about seventeen or eighteen, judging by the sparse moustache he was trying to grow, asked nervously, 'How tough's tough?'

As Tania went to answer, she heard a whistling and rushing sound overhead. Before she had time to look up, a bomb landed amidships, squarely in the centre of the barge. The blast lifted her and her two companions off their feet, and for a brief moment they found themselves flying through the air.

The shock of hitting the icy river brought them to their senses. They knew they'd last only a few minutes unless they reached land safely. But where was land!

The three of them struck out for the shore, struggling to keep their heads above water as the current carried them farther and farther from the bank.

This was it, the moment Tania had dreaded. It was one thing being shot or blown up – hopefully, you wouldn't know much about it. But drowning in Mother Volga, her own Russian river, with seconds that seemed like hours to go over your sixteen years – that was the worst possible fate.

FORTY

Tania was a strong swimmer. But swimming in the warm, still water of the Pioneer swimming baths was one thing; battling against ice and current in waves that swept over her head and down her throat was beyond her. The freezing waters soon numbed her will to survive. Then the realisation that she was drowning brought her to her senses, and she struck out desperately, kicking and flailing like a windmill.

It was no good. The river was winning, dragging her head below the waves.

All at once, she felt rough hands grab her by the hair and haul her out of the water. The older Siberian had managed to scramble on to an ice floe, and was trying to pull out Tania and his young comrade. First one, then the other, until all three were clinging to the slippery block of ice.

'Th-th-thanks,' she managed to say, as she rode the icy roller-coaster.

But it was only a temporary respite. For the ice floe was careering downstream like a panicky horse, knocking aside anything in its way. It was so cold, her hands stuck fast to the ice; every time she tore a hand away, she left skin behind.

If they didn't drown, they'd certainly freeze to death.

Suddenly the floe struck a sandbank. Like a beached whale it thrashed about, turning this way and that, rolling over and over until, finally, it broke free and continued on its way. In the few moments of struggle, however, it had shaken off its unwanted passengers. The three swiftly slipped from its back on to the sandbar, and there they lay, half-frozen, half-conscious.

It was the older man, Ivan, who once more took the initiative. Pulling his companions to their feet, he forced them along the stretch of ice-encrusted sand with prods and punches that kept them moving and their blood circulating.

'Come on, Boris! And you, girl! You sad sons of bitches! Shift yourselves!'

Somehow they slipped and slithered to the west bank of the river, not knowing or even caring whether they were in enemy or home territory.

Near the end of the sandbar was a large concrete pipe, emptying its waste into the river. By the smell they knew at once it must be a city sewer. Whose sewage it was – Russian or German – mattered not.

Ivan muttered, through chattering teeth, 'All sh-shit st-stinks the s-s-same!'

'No!' Tania said firmly between clenched teeth. 'I'm not going in there!'

'Suit yourself,' said Ivan, taking shelter inside the tunnel.

Boris joined him and, shortly after, so did Tania. Standing inside the pipe, she started to regain some warmth, and she wrung out her sodden clothes.

'Just for a moment,' she said, shivering. 'But not a step farther. God, it s-s-stinks!'

'We don't have much choice, do we?' said Ivan. 'It's either back to the freezing river or take a chance in this sewer.'

'It must lead somewhere,' his mate offered.

'Yeah, if we last that long,' Tania groaned, 'wallowing in filth, with rats eating us alive.'

'Well, look at it this way,' said Ivan savagely. 'It's either a swift death in the river or a slow choke to death in the tunnel.'

'At least we've a chance of surviving in the sewer,' the younger man said. 'We might reach safety before our lungs give out.'

'Then what?' said Tania sourly. 'Get our heads blown off once we poke them above ground?'

'Suit yourself,' Ivan grunted.

He started off down the tunnel, trudging through a thick, stinking river of human waste which clung to his boots and trousers. Boris followed.

The choice was Tania's: river or sewer, sink or swim. Sink in filth or swim in icy water. She was retching from the stench. Oh well, she thought, safety in numbers. She set off after them, pinching her nose and breathing through her mouth.

Their splashing, squelching footsteps echoed eerily as they felt their way along the slimy sewer. The farther they went, the dimmer grew the light. Soon they were stumbling along blindly.

Now and then they heard the squeals and tiny pattering feet of the sewer's tenants. But something else posed a far greater danger: poisonous fumes. Their one desperate hope was that they'd come to a manhole cover or steps leading to a sewage treatment station. The dream that kept them going was of sweet, fresh air, lung-loads of it.

With any luck, they'd come up in safe territory and make it back to their own lines. It was about the same odds as a peashooter outshooting a howitzer.

FORTY-ONE

After half an hour, Ivan began to flag. 'It's my asthma,' he wheezed.

More than once they had to stop for him to get his breath. He would bury his nose in his wet jacket and wave them on.

'You go on. I need to rest.'

When at last he passed out, Boris would have abandoned him. But Tania refused.

'He rescued us from the river. We must try to save him.'

They tried to pull him along between them. But even Tania had to admit it was hopeless: they were near to exhaustion themselves, and feeling extremely sick, what with the slippery slime and sludge sucking at their feet, and the foul air that made them light-headed.

There was nothing for it but to leave Ivan behind – the man who'd saved their lives. Tania knelt down beside him in the filth, daring to meet his eyes.

'Forgive us, Ivan. We have no choice…'

He slowly nodded and waved her away.

They left him sitting in the filth, his head propped against the wall.

The two battled on in silence for another half an hour, their steps getting slower, heavier. Pressing their noses tightly into their jackets, they breathed only through their mouths. Even so, the cloying stench forced its way up their noses and down their throats, burning the walls of their lungs.

All at once Boris let out a muffled cry. Tania's first thought was that he'd been attacked by a starving rat. But, no, his hand had brushed something hard and sharp on the tunnel wall. The tiniest glimmer of light shone above their heads. As their eyes grew accustomed to the lighter shade of darkness, they made out metal rungs on the wall – leading upwards, through a funnel.

Hope squeezed out the last ounces of their strength, enabling them to haul themselves up, step by step, to the very top. The faint light formed a circular halo above their heads. It must be a manhole cover.

With both hands, Boris thrust upwards: once, twice, three times. The cover wouldn't budge. It was rusted over for want of use, sealed by the dirt and frost of years.

So near and yet so far. Surely a mere manhole cover wouldn't defeat them now? No, no, no! They had to shift it. Tania clambered up, squeezing behind Boris and wedging her body against the funnel wall, so that she could hold herself with her feet and push with her arms.

'One, two, three, heave! One, two, three, heave! One, two, three, *heave!*'

At the third attempt, the cover suddenly shifted with a crack like a gunshot, snapping the dirt-filled seal. One more heave, and it moved aside with a resounding clank.

'*Aaargh. Aaahhh-aaahhh!*'

Never had the smoky, putrid air of war-torn Stalingrad smelled so sweet. They lay there, half-in, half-out, gulping down the cool air, emptying their lungs of poison and re-filling them with life. But the freezing air seared and scorched their throat and lungs, forcing them to take shorter breaths.

The bright sunlight made them screw their eyes tight like moles. For the moment they wouldn't have cared even if they'd been staring down the barrel of an enemy gun – just as long as they could breathe in the fresh air.

After a few minutes they'd recovered enough to narrow their eyes into narrow slits and peer about.

Oh no!

Across the street was a group of soldiers in field-green uniforms and forage caps. They were standing in a queue, evidently waiting for lunch, judging by their billy cans and the appetising aroma of hot food.

'Ours or theirs?' whispered Boris.

'Dunno,' Tania murmured.

She couldn't care whether the soldiers were friend or foe. Food had no homeland: German *Tee* would be as welcome as Russian *chai*.

FORTY-TWO

They didn't have to wait long. As the bedraggled sewer rats tagged on the back of the queue and passed inside the canteen, the soldier in front suddenly whipped round, holding his nose.

'*Gott in Himmel! Was ist das?*'

Tania nudged Boris, warning him to keep his mouth shut.

Nervous as a kitten, she smiled sweetly at the German and held up her filthy hands as if she'd been engaged on some sensitive mission. That seemed to satisfy him. He turned about, shuffling his feet forward and hustling those in front. Boris and Tania kept their place at the end of the line, moving along with the others.

At the counter, they grabbed a tray and spare mess tins, holding them out for soup and bread. A big beefy cook, a Ukrainian Hilfi or 'helper', by the look of him, splashed a watery cabbage soup into their tins. For Tania, he fished out a lump of fatty meat from the bottom of the tureen.

She summoned up one of the few German words she remembered from school:

'*Danke.*'

The cook smiled broadly, waving a hand at the half-slices of greyish-brown bread and the urn of hot tea.

They searched for an empty table. Only on the far side were there spaces. They made for them and nervously joined four German sappers chatting and laughing among themselves. None of them paid the two newcomers any attention until first one, then the others stopped chewing on their bread. Raising their noses, they sniffed the air.

'Pooh!' one exclaimed, casting accusing looks at his friends. The others laughed, as if to say, 'Don't look at me.'

Looking round, they glanced at Tania, not believing a young girl capable of such a vile smell. She too wrinkled her nose in disgust, apparently blaming the stink on someone else. Everyone stared at Boris, bending his head low over the soup.

'*Schweinhund!*' yelled one of the Germans.

The hubbub reached the ears of a passing officer, who took one look at the two intruders and recognised their uniforms, despite the filth.

'Hey, you!' he shouted in Russian. 'Name and number!'

The game was up. But before the officer could act, an old man in a long white cook's apron, wearing a black waistcoat and homespun shirt, hurried over. His long beard and deeply wrinkled face gave him authority.

'It's all right, Captain,' he said in Russian. 'These are Hilfswillige, working for the German army. I can vouch for them.'

Tania recognised him at once. It was the old

Studebaker driver, Granddad Timofei! But what was he doing here?

The officer seemed unconvinced. But he confined himself to ordering Tania and Boris out of the mess hall, before they gave German food a bad name.

Timofei led them into the kitchen where they were out of German hearing. All the kitchen staff were local people, peeling potatoes, swilling out slops, 'confiscating' vegetables, eggs and chickens from yards in the suburbs, and slaving over hot stoves from morning to night.

'Phew!' old Timofei cried, searching for his nose amidst the unkempt foliage of whiskers. 'Have you taken a dip in the sewers?'

There was no point in denying it. Tania started to tell their story. But he cut her short.

'What the eye doesn't see, the heart doesn't grieve over, eh? But... what the nose smells, vermin of all sorts come investigating. Get my meaning?'

He was right. Someone was bound to arrive soon, following their noses.

'Get rid of those clothes and scrub that stink off your bodies,' ordered Timofei. 'Use the tap over there above the washing-up trough. Tania, I'll rig up a screen for you.'

While he trundled a divider across one of the washing-up troughs, she quickly undressed, tossing her filthy snow-suit, boots and undies into the swill bin. Even though the tap water was cold, it was far warmer than what she'd recently experienced. She put her head under the tap and scrubbed her hair, face, shoulders, back, stomach, legs and feet with a large lump of carbolic.

A wrinkled hand appeared over the divider top, draping a new set of clothes on the rail. They were far too big, but how lovely to pull on fresh-smelling, baggy overalls, a white skull cap and slip-on sandals!

From barge to river to ice-floe to sewer… and now this – a warm, clean kitchen. The only snag was… it was German.

She thought sadly of Ivan who'd saved her life. She couldn't help feeling guilty about leaving him behind. Two of them had survived – for how long was anybody's guess.

FORTY-THREE

Boris was all for making a run for it. But he was still wet behind the ears, with no experience of battle. Tania was more cautious.

'No, Borya, we must wait. It won't help anyone if we're caught and shot.'

Half an hour later, the officer hardly recognised the two little cherubims, with their glowing pink cheeks, smoothed-down hair and white robes.

After a brief interrogation, using Timofei as interpreter, he was satisfied they were deserters who were eager to fight for the Germans. He left them in the old man's custody, with a stern warning to Timofei:

'Your life depends on their good behaviour!'

Tania was keen to ask old Timofei whose side he was on. Even when talking to him on the trip to Rodimtsev's camp, she had never suspected him of going over to the enemy. But he was clearly accepted here by the German officers, who referred to him as 'Herr Yarkov', and by the kitchen staff, who preferred the respectful 'Timofei Petrovich'.

Perhaps he was a spy for the Germans and the Russians! Not that he would admit it. After all, he had not questioned Tania too closely about her movements since they'd last met.

Boris and Tania now had to be found accommodation. Their fond hopes of sleeping by the warm kitchen stoves were soon dashed. All the kitchen Hilfis lived 'at home' – that is to say, they disappeared each night who knows where.

Timofei explained:

'Underground are whole tribes of children, waiting for the Hilfis to come. They survive on scraps and water smuggled out of the German kitchens. Little does Fritz know he's feeding half the city! Those with no relatives or friends working for the Germans have to fend for themselves, and usually die a slow death.'

So, for the time being, the ruins became home to Boris and Tania. But if they were to survive the cold, they would need more than cook's overalls. Old Timofei persuaded the German quartermaster to issue them with padded jackets and trousers, rabbit fur gloves and hats and strong army boots. Given the high death rate, there were always more uniforms than bodies to clothe.

The winter clothes were a life-saver. Snowflakes twirled slowly down through the air; the morning frosts of November caught the throat and turned each breath to icy mist. Unprotected ears and noses would soon whiten with frostbite and, unless protected, have to be cut off.

Colliding ice floes made such a loud crack and rumble, they could be heard right across the city, putting fear into German hearts – for soon the Volga would freeze over completely, forming a thousand paths for Russian tanks and lorries.

This might offer an escape route for Boris and Tania. If they could just make it to the river, they might find their way by night to a Russian post. But they owed it to Granddad Timofei to stay put for the moment. If they escaped, he'd probably be shot.

Now that the two were billeted on the 'underground people', Tania was itching to meet these men and women, regarded as traitors by the Russians, who helped the enemy. They would certainly be shot if caught, and they must have known it. Did they do it willingly, or did they have no choice? What would Tania's mother have done about children starving to death before her eyes? Maybe Tania shouldn't judge them too harshly. After all, they were giving her shelter, until she could escape.

While Boris was led off to his lodgings, Tania stayed with Aunt Moosya, in the cellar of what had until recently been a new eight-storey tenement – eight storeys which had taken a year to build and a minute to knock down. Eight tall, proud floors reduced to rubble. Where had they gone – those walls and windows, ceilings and floors, beds and bodies? It was as if some man-mountain had stepped on them and pounded them to dust.

Aunt Moosya was one of those peasant women whose life had made her old before her time. She covered her shapeless form with layers of ragged shawls, jumpers and skirts taken from the dead bodies of her neighbours. Added to this outer cladding were tasselled tablecloths and velvet curtains knotted about her waist and draped over her shoulders.

Aunt Moosya was a survivor. She traded valuables – gold rings, watches, earrings, red stars, even gold teeth – for food, clothing and fuel for her little stove. The German booty was not so much for herself as for the six hungry orphans she cared for in her den. They all slept on plank beds, two to a bunk, one above the other.

When Tania first arrived, Aunt Moosya waved her arms about and beat her breast, wailing, 'Lord Almighty! Where am I going to put her? No, no! No room. Clear off!'

Old Timofei waited for the storm to blow over before producing a sweetener: a sack of sunflower seeds. Aunt Moosya continued to protest, but now through teeth that expertly cracked the seeds and spat out the husks. Timofei and Aunt Moosya haggled. Finally, they shook hands on a deal: Tania, in exchange for the sack of sunflower seeds, half a salami and a bag of flour.

Like most citizens of the deep who'd had their ears battered by bombs falling night and day, Aunt Moosya was partially deaf, so any conversation with her was loud enough to be heard by eavesdroppers.

'Take Stassya's place, girl,' she shouted in her sing-song peasant voice. 'Bottom shelf. Stassya can snuggle up with me.'

Tania was glad of any resting place, even a wooden plank that stank of wee. Night, however, wasn't sleeping time for all Aunt Moosya's orphans. Two of the older boys went about mysterious business under cover of darkness. Tania thought it best not to ask too many questions of these artful dodgers.

FORTY-FOUR

As Tania lay back on her hard bunk, she watched Aunt Moosya bent over the stove, mixing her precious wheat flour with bits of old turnip and apple peel, dried peas and mushrooms.

'Aunt Moosya,' she called. 'Are there many kids left in the city?'

The woman shrugged.

'God knows. There are bound to be lots of little mites running wild. They don't understand war, friend or foe.' She crossed herself with two fingers before rushing on, glad of someone to talk to.

'The Germans use kids for running errands – you know, like filling their water bottles.'

Tania snorted.

'Are they too lazy to fill the bottles themselves?'

'No-o-oo. Too dangerous, what with them snipers sniping.'

Aunt Moosya evidently didn't approve of snipers.

'For a crust of bread, Fritz gets them kiddies to fill water bottles from the river.'

'Isn't that risky?'

'Like a fox in a hen-house! *Snip-snap*, they're gone. Commissars shoot kids who fetch water for Fritzes. Tsar Stalin, he says: kill anyone who helps Germans.

Shoot first, ask questions afterwards.'

Tania's stomach churned. Yet she felt she had to stick up for Soviet soldiers. After all, she was one herself, a sniper who might be ordered to shoot little children – even her own brothers, if they worked for the Germans.

'War's war. I bet the Germans shoot kids who act as scouts for our side.'

Aunt Moosya sighed.

'Our side, their side, front side, back side. It's all the same. Me? I'm on my side, trying to keep going and save orphan kids.'

She put down her bowl and growled, 'Of course them Fritzes shoot kiddies as young as four or five, just for nicking stuff. God help the poor souls caught spying. They string 'em up in the main streets, so's everyone can get an eyeful.'

Tania had seen and heard some terrible things in recent months. But to leave children dangling on a rope for people to stare at...

'As a matter of fact, there's a hanging tomorrow,' said Aunt Moosya grimly. 'Poor little fellow. Brave, though. And as crafty as a wagon-load of monkeys. Do you know what he did? Went and offered his services to the Fritzes as a cobbler. "Mender of bad soles" he called himself. And d'you know why? So's he could steal secrets. What do you think of that?'

A cold hand was squeezing Tania's throat. Her brother Misha's hobby was mending boots and shoes. He could cut out leather soles and tack them on to worn-out footwear just like a master cobbler. She knew the phrase 'Mender of bad soles' only too well – she'd memorised it from a Shakespeare play, *Julius Caesar,* and had often quoted it to Misha.

Aunt Moosya babbled on, 'The young daredevil went from company to company mending hundreds of pairs of German boots with his hammer and wooden shoe last. He became a sort of mascot – they called him their *Schuhmacherlein*. Quite a favourite, he was. And, do you know, all the while he was filching secret documents from the officers' desks and filing cabinets, stuffing them down his shirt and taking them through the lines. The poor old Germans! They never suspected the little cobbler of being the reason why snipers were picking off the officers one by one.

'Of course, he had his accomplices – a couple of thirteen-year olds, a boy and a girl. One moment they'd be playing hopscotch in the street, innocent as the day is young, the next they'd be dashing from one command post to the other, right across the battle lines.'

'What happened?' Tania asked.

'What happened? *Gospodee!* What do you think? They got caught, of course. The three of them were walking along by the German HQ. Next thing they know, a platoon appears out of nowhere and descends on them like a plague of locusts. Too late to make a run for it.'

Aunt Moosya sighed deeply.

'It was bound to happen sooner or later. The little cobbler and his apprentices got themselves well and truly hammered on their own last. And that was that.'

'Do you know their names?' Tania asked. She dreaded the reply.

'Names? No, just Little Master Cobbler.'

'Where's the hanging?'

'What?'

'I said, where will they be hanged?'

'Bryanskaya Street, over by Orlovka. D'you know it?'

'Vaguely,' Tania said. 'What time?'

'Around four, so I hear.'

Tania turned to face the wall. Hot tears were running down her cheeks. But maybe it wasn't Misha. He might be safe, playing football with Vanya far behind the lines, without a thought of Germans, war or spying.

There was only one way to find out: she would have to go to the hanging.

FORTY-FIVE

The next day, Old Timofei found odd jobs for the two newcomers in the kitchen. Boris did his work reluctantly, anxious to get away. If the Red Army discovered he'd collaborated with the enemy, he could be dragged before a firing squad. It was all Tania could do to hold him back.

'Look,' she whispered, 'if we go now, we sign Timofei's death warrant; he's responsible for us. Don't forget, he saved our lives.'

'That's his look-out,' retorted Boris. 'I came to Stalingrad to fight, not to peel potatoes for Hitlerites.'

'Calm down, Borya. I'll work something out. To tell you the truth, I've another reason for staying.' And she told him about her brother.

'But you don't know it's him, do you?' he said.

'No, but I have to find out.'

Tania now had to seek Timofei's permission to take time off. Once he learned the reason, he was sympathetic. Yet there was something that told her he knew more than he was letting on. A few more lines appeared among the wrinkles on his face.

'Go with God,' he said. 'But be back for supper.'

As she turned to go, he called after her, 'Tanechka. Be brave!'

Boris insisted on accompanying Tania to the outskirts

of town, where Bryanskaya Street crosses the Little Wet Mosque stream. A dozen elderly men and women had already gathered on a snow-covered patch of ground with a lone acacia tree in the centre. They were standing quietly, heads bowed, as at a funeral.

All at once, a procession came down the road; the crowd heard the tramping boots before they saw the twenty soldiers. They were marching in step on either side of three children, two boys and a girl, walking barefoot through the snow.

Tania recognised the fair-haired boy at once. He was the shortest of the three. He held his head high and his lips were moving, as if singing to himself. She caught the wavering words: *Sheeroka strana moya rodnaya* – 'Wide is my native land'. The other two took up the song and their shrill voices rose above the crunching boots. She fought to hold back the tears.

Then, 'Misha!'

Startled by her voice, he stared around, a bewildered look on his pale face. Suddenly he caught sight of his sister. He stopped singing and stumbled, as a soldier shoved him from behind.

What? Why? How? The questions were printed on his puzzled face. He gave a slight shrug and pursed his lips, as if embarrassed to be seen like this. Then he put on the cheeky grin she knew so well.

'Tania!' he shouted out, 'give my love to Mum and Dad!'

She ran alongside the soldiers and reached past them,

touching his ice-cold arm. As he squeezed her hand, one of the guards knocked her aside with the butt of his rifle.

There was nothing she could do but watch numbly as the procession halted on the barren land. The soldiers flung three lengths of rope over the branches of the tree, two on either side and one in the middle. The platoon sergeant put a noose round each of the children's heads and tightened the knot beneath their left ears.

The three youngsters were silent, heads bowed. Suddenly, in the silence, Misha's voice pierced the frosty air saying the words all Russian children knew so well from their Pioneer book. He spoke them clearly, his head flung back, looking towards his sister.

'You only live once. And you should live your life so that, when you die, you can say: I gave everything for my people.'

The sergeant waited for him to finish before giving a sharp order. The soldiers hoisted up the three children.

Tania stared. Mercifully, tears veiled the final scene. All she saw, as through a rain-spattered window-pane, was a fair head bent to one side and two legs swinging gently, like stockings on a clothes line.

Sobs racked her whole body and she fell to the ground shrieking, 'Misha! Misha! Misha!'

The German soldiers formed up and marched away.

The bystanders lingered for a moment, uncertain what to do next. Then the old men and women shuffled off into the gathering gloom, and soon Bryanskaya Street was deserted – apart from the snow-swept ground with its leafless acacia tree and the three dangling bodies. Powdered snow was already settling on their hair and eyebrows, a chill wind gently swaying the figures like catkins on a willow tree.

Tania stood up, pulled herself together and stepped towards the tree. With both hands she reached up and grasped her brother's icy feet.

'You need some shoes,' she murmured, 'my little mender of bad soles.'

FORTY-SIX

Tania trudged away through the snow.

She felt proud of her brother; war brings out unfathomable courage. Yet to die at twelve! Never again would those blue eyes smile softly at her, give a crafty wink when he was naughty, fill with tears when Mum told him off. They were closed now, for ever.

The more she reflected on Misha's life and death, the more determined Tania was that he should not have died in vain. She would see to that. If she'd had any remaining doubts about killing, Misha's bravery had removed them. Now she would kill for him, revenge his death.

'Boris,' she said, breaking the sombre silence, 'we're going back. Tonight.'

Her tone of voice was final. Boris smiled to himself. He thought it unkind to remind her of their debt to Timofei. But the thought hadn't escaped Tania. She consoled herself that he, like Aunt Moosya, was a survivor. He'd understand: she had a job to do.

'We won't go back to the kitchens,' she said. 'We'll lie low till nightfall and follow the stream down to the Volga. As far as I remember, it comes out somewhere between Spartakovka and the Tractor Plant. If we can make it to the Plant, we should be safe.'

Boris accepted her command naturally. She might be only a schoolgirl, but she was a seasoned fighter. This was her city.

'What will we do for weapons?' he asked.

'Weapons?' she said, as if she had already considered it. 'We have weapons. Teeth, fists and feet, hard heads and loud voices. Have you ever wrung the neck of a chicken? Germans' necks are no different.'

A few moments later, she added, 'We're wearing German uniform, aren't we? With any luck, a passing patrol will take us for Hilfis because we're on their territory, and they won't expect us to speak their lingo.'

It was getting dark. Despite the padded jackets, a damp wind pierced their clothes and made them shiver. Tania filled her lungs with fresh night air and looked up at the starry sky. The Great Bear was looking down upon Mamayev Kurgan. The big round moon was shining brightly on friend and foe alike. To the right, probably over Red October, a dozen rockets lit up the sky, spilling into a golden rain of sparks and shooting stars. For the moment, there was no shooting.

A derelict boathouse stood before them, its porch overhanging the frozen stream; a half-sunken rowing boat reared up in the ice.

'We'll wait there,' she said. 'In a few hours it'll be safer to move.'

The boathouse offered a windshield, but it stank to high heaven. They cleared a space of splintered timbers and empty cans in one corner. It was cramped and

Tania's feet soon went to sleep. Boris had some breadcrumbs in his jacket pocket, so they shared a few mouthfuls.

After chewing in silence for a while, Boris asked a strange question.

'Tania, is it true that Hitler only has one eye?'

'I don't know, Boris. As far as I know, he's got both his eyes.'

'I heard a soldier say he only had one eye and only one testicle – so he can't have children.'

'I wouldn't know about that,' she said. She could feel herself blushing at the thought. But what a relief for the world if Hitler couldn't produce little monsters like himself.

'I read somewhere,' continued Boris, 'that Hitler was gassed in the Great War, and that he isn't German at all, but Austrian. Even his name's false: he's not 'Adolf Hitler', he's something beginning with 'Sh'.'

'Schickelgruber,' she said. She'd read that in a school book.

'Is it true that he was only a corporal? That's what our commissar told us.'

'As far as I know.'

'Well, how can you rise through the ranks to become a big boss, a Führer? I thought our commissar was having us on.'

'Commissars don't lie,' Tania said sternly. She decided it was time to change the subject.

'Have you been in the army long, Boris?'

'Oh, ages. Since September '41.'

'That's only three months.'

'It seems like a lifetime.'

Boris suddenly broke off.

'Did you hear that?'

'What?'

Tania strained her ears. The noise was coming closer and closer, from the direction of the Volga.

'It's ours, don't worry,' she said.

The drone came steadily closer.

FORTY-SEVEN

The plane was circling overhead, making certain of its position. The Germans started firing at it from the other side of the stream; they didn't use searchlights because it was flying too low to be caught in a beam.

It was making a second circle before dropping its bombs. They made a clattering noise, like pop-guns, over the German trenches near the far bank.

One more circle, and the little plywood plane tried again. This time – right on the button. The explosions were so close, Boris and Tania had to cover their heads. A few pieces of shrapnel flew over them. Then a piece fell – right between them. It was small and jagged and too hot to pick up,.

Tania thanked her lucky stars. It could so easily have gone straight through her heart.

Then, unexpectedly – *trrr-trrr-trrr* – right above their heads. They could feel the draught as the bullets whizzed by.

Where had that machine-gun come from? And why was it firing at the boathouse?

Tania raised her head to peer out of the window. There was silence all round. The plane was now chugging away somewhere behind them. All at once, she felt a sneeze coming on... She squeezed her nose with her fingers as hard as she could, and rubbed the bridge of her nose. When the sneeze had passed, she muttered, 'Let's get out of here!'

Just as they were climbing out of the boathouse, the bombardment opened up. Single bullets whistled and slapped against the boathouse walls and bounced off the frozen stream. Multi-coloured tracer bullets criss-crossed each other in the sky. To their left they could hear grenades exploding; to the right, shells were going off.

They quickly dodged back, when a mortar landed close by, almost deafening them. As Tania flattened herself on the floor, something heavy fell on her from behind and slowly slid to one side. It was Boris, clutching his stomach. In the light of the moon, she watched his face turn white and his mauve lips press tightly together.

'They got me...'

He tried to smile. Blood was seeping from beneath his jacket. Great drops of sweat appeared on his forehead.

'I... Tania...'

His lips were moving, but it was impossible to catch any words. With one last painful effort he attempted to raise himself, then fell back.

Tania stared at him, shocked. How could he? Only a moment earlier he had been telling her about Siberia. He couldn't be dead!

What was she to do? She couldn't just leave him there.

She went through his pockets, taking out a penknife, scraps of newspaper for making cigarettes, his identity card and a single sheet of paper folded like a paper boat.

She smoothed it out. Crooked, childish writing filled the page – it was from his wife.

How odd. He hadn't mentioned a wife.

Borya, Dearest!
We miss you terribly, and we're waiting for the war to end so you can come home. Galochka is a big girl now and can already walk by herself – she hardly ever falls over...

Tania read the letter to the end. It wasn't long – greetings from his parents, a few words about work, hope for a swift victory over the Fascists. At the end, two unsteady lines drawn by a child's hand guided by the mother; and under this,

Galochka wrote this all by herself.

Tania gazed sadly at Galochka's father, his jacket torn open. On his muscular, nut-brown chest was a tattoo of a red heart pierced by a blue dagger. He was lying there as helpless as a stricken sparrow, and on his face was an apologetic smile.

'Boris,' she said quietly, 'I'll write to your wife and daughter, I promise.' But what would she say? Boris is dead. What else? Boris died before having a chance to fight. She'd hardly known him; he was a comrade-in-arms, one of many, far too many, who'd died while she herself had survived.

In far-off Yakutsk, untouched by bombs and bullets,

the words *Boris Danilov is dead* would not just be words: they'd be a tragedy, the end of hope. And reading them, a wife would no longer have a husband, a little girl would no longer have a father.

No. Tania wanted the letter she wrote to be from someone grieving as much as those who would read the letter. Then it might not hurt so much. People sometimes need to be lied to. They passionately want a hero's death for the man they loved. They want him not to have died an ordinary death, but to have done something special. And, above all, they want to believe that he remembered them before he died.

Putting the little paper boat into her pocket, Tania made up her mind. She'd say that she and Boris had served together for some time, that he'd died a hero during night fighting in Stalingrad (which was true), that before dying he'd shot three Germans (which wasn't true). And that before he died in her arms, he had remembered his wife and daughter, Galochka: his last wish had been that his daughter should never forget her father.

That was the least she could do.

FORTY-EIGHT

As Tania crawled out of the boathouse, she cursed the bright wintry moon. It shone like a spotlight, catching her in its beam and exposing her to the full view of those who'd gunned down Boris. The wind continued to bluster along the stream's open banks, cold and relentless. It blocked Tania's nose and blurred her eyes.

Underfoot the hard snow made each step mew and squeak like a cat chasing mice. It was impossible to muffle her footsteps or blend into the shadows. But the only Germans she came upon appeared to be sleeping peacefully in the snow. The red-nosed frost, not bullets, had done for them.

Welcome to the Russian winter, *Mein Herr!* thought Tania.

Her dim memory of the stream's course – Mum had taken her to see Grandma's new flat in Spartakovka five years back – served her true. Once she reached safety, she intended to surrender to the Red Army troops, to explain away her German uniform and demand to be taken directly to General Rodimtsev.

However, Aunt Moosya's words about 'Tsar' Stalin's order filled her ears: 'Shoot first, ask questions afterwards!'

Half an hour later she was approaching the outer limits

of the Tractor Plant. To her left was the shadowy housing estate of Spartakovka – just the tenement foundations, now laid bare. Leaving the frozen stream, she ran, bent double, towards a sentry-box where, in peacetime, security staff – depending on how sober they were – raised and lowered a red and white boom.

Tania's heart was in her mouth; she expected to hear a crack at any moment, to feel a sharp pain and fall down dead. She ran as if trying to beat the world record for the hundred metres. Just keep going, don't trip up, faster, faster!

She made it, clean out of breath. The little wooden hut was quiet and in darkness, evidently deserted. But just as she was mounting the steps, she ran straight into a guard. He was as startled as she was.

For a split second they both froze with fear. But he had one big advantage. He was armed.

'*Hande hoch!*' he barked, waving a pistol in Tania's face.

The hated German voice triggered off a reaction in her brain. What were the combat moves they'd taught her at training school?

Quick as a flash, she chopped his pistol-wielding arm with the blunt part of her right hand. His pistol went clattering down the steps into the roadway. Then she lashed out as hard as she could with her boot, kicking him where it hurt most. Fortunately for her, he was a skinny young fellow with glasses, unfamiliar with martial arts. As he doubled over, losing his spectacles, she put a neck hold on him, squeezing his windpipe. If she wasn't strong enough to break his neck, she'd cut off his air supply. Kill him! Kill! Kill!

What was it she'd told Boris? Strangling Germans was as easy as wringing a chicken's neck... What she hadn't said was that the German had to be no bigger than a chicken. This one was a head taller than her. He sank his teeth into her hand, and she let go for a split second.

Then the memory of Misha gave Tania strength she didn't know she possessed. She fought with the fury of the desperate. It was him or her. Yet she knew she couldn't hold out much longer. She had to kill him quickly, or else... Panic seized her.

Now it was the sentry who had her in a stranglehold. Tania gasped. She could feel herself drifting in and out of consciousness. Another moment, and she'd pass out, leaving him to shoot or choke her to death.

Dimly, far, far away, she heard voices. Were they Russian? At the same time, the fingers round her neck relaxed, then fell away. She staggered back against the wall.

A Russian patrol, hearing the scuffle, had burst in and pulled the sentry off... just in time. A burly Red Army-man smashed his rifle butt down on the German's head – once, twice, three times, until he squirmed no more.

It was the closest Tania had come to death, and it was several minutes before she got her breath back.

FORTY-NINE

As her brain slowly cleared, Tania could hear her rescuers discussing what to do with her. Meanwhile, all she could do was grunt: her swollen throat blocked the way to words.

One thing was obvious: like the German, they didn't realise she was a girl. Nor did they know she was Russian.

'A couple of thieves having a barney!' spat one soldier in disgust.

'You'd think he'd pick on someone his own size,' said another.

'What'll we do with the little Fritz? Take him in and see if he'll sing?'

'No, shoot the bastard! Sarge said take no prisoners, didn't he?'

A strangled cry brought their discussion to an abrupt end. Tania had finally found her voice.

'Russian... sniper...' She croaked out each word over her aching tonsils.

Her outburst brought a stay of execution. Only when the soldiers found no weapons or means of identity on her did they decide against a bullet in the head. Instead, they marched her off for their superiors to deal with.

The route back to Russian lines was long and tortuous. It skirted the Tractor Plant, which was almost entirely in enemy hands, and involved a wide detour along the river. The two-week-old ice no longer gave way underfoot, and the moon lit up a network of well-trodden paths and countless sled traces.

The man whose rifle butt had cracked open the German skull ran on ahead surely and swiftly, as if he'd spent his entire life covering these criss-crossed tracks. Now and then, as the ice started to crack and open out into a wide ice-hole, he'd slide to a halt, muttering to himself, 'Whoops! Wrong way. Should've turned right.' And off the patrol would hurry again, to the right or left, follow my leader.

The sullen moon suddenly disappeared behind a cloud. They now had to pick their way round shell-stricken barges frozen in the ice, and over thick ropes that glinted icy blue, rearing up steeply over the bows of ice-bound launches.

The dry, stuttering cough of a machine-gun followed the patrol. Here and there they heard the *ping* and *nee-yow* of bullets on ice, and saw spurts of freshly-fallen snow rise and fall in rows as if by magic. Each crack and spurt made every nerve in Tania's body tingle. But the patrol kept out of range. The men were clearly experienced at making this nightly sortie into what they called the 'bear's parlour', to blow up his supplies. Their white hooded cloaks helped conceal them against snow and ice; only their grey fur hats with ear flaps presented a target – a mere pinhead when seen from two hundred metres away.

Finally, after several hours, the patrol arrived back at base. Tania was dropping from exhaustion. They reported on orders carried out, on enemy strength and deployment. And they handed over the prisoner in her grey-green uniform and rabbit-fur hat – obviously relieved to be rid of this unwanted burden.

Like his men, the commanding officer wasn't happy about taking responsibility for Tania's fate, all the more so when she rapped out the names of generals and officers she knew personally.

'My commanding officer is General Rodimtsev,' she said. 'My father, Ivan Belov, is Commissar and I'm with Lieutenant Zaitsev's special sniper unit.'

Her assurance convinced the officer she was telling the truth. Even if she weren't, he didn't fancy being shot for killing a spy.

The walk to divisional headquarters did not take long. When the escorting officer delivered his prisoner, Zaitsev immediately vouched for her. He made no sign as to whether he was glad to see her or not, nor did he ask about her absence. His attention, like that of the other snipers, was focused on the briefing being given by Major-General Gurtiev, Rodimtsev's deputy.

Tania, standing at the back for the briefing, was overjoyed to be back home with her 'family'. Lena gave her a broad smile, Salami winked in greeting, and Tolya waved both hands clenched together.

Gurtiev was giving final instructions, tapping a sketch pinned to a board.

'Our target is a five-storey tenement. It's of strategic importance to us since it overlooks the Volga. If we can knock out enemy positions and take the building, we'll cut down attacks on the main river ferry.'

All eyes were on the map, which was covered in red, blue and yellow markers. Red for light-machine-gun on the second floor, blue for a pair of snipers on the third, yellow for a heavy mortar on the ground floor.

Soviet forces were to storm the building with every weapon they had: mortars, grenades, high-velocity rifles, even heavy batteries from the far side of the river – all co-ordinated by a system of light signals and field telephones.

'Understood?' asked Gurtiev.

'Understood,' they all chorused back.

'Then get to work. Best of luck!'

As Gurtiev left, Zaitsev made a bee-line for Tania.

'Good,' he rapped. 'I'm glad you're back. Now – back to work.'

No 'Where have you been? How do you feel?' He had no interest in how close to death she'd come in the icy river, in the stifling sewer, in the enemy mess hall. What did he care about her feelings at Misha's hanging, or the shell that had ripped open Boris's guts? He wasn't worried that a German might have strangled the life out of her. Nothing concerned him, save her return.

Yet it was Zaitsev who had advised Rodimtsev she needed toughening up. It was Zaitsev who'd put her through hell. He had ice for a heart.

Her comrades crowded round when Zaitsev had gone, peppering her with questions. In the meantime, Tolya brought her an enamel mug of hot tea and rye rusks. Between mouthfuls she did her best to fill them in, though she was desperately tired. In the end, she collapsed through sheer exhaustion, and Tolya had to carry her to a wooden bunk behind a curtain.

Through a dense fog of tiredness she heard the words, 'We'll give you a shake at one o'clock. That'll give you six hours' sleep.'

Lena's quiet voice added, 'You'll need it, after what you've been through.'

For the first time since she'd slept on Aunt Moosya's rough planks, Tania fell into a sleep that even mortars and bombs couldn't penetrate.

FIFTY

When Tania awoke, she realised the sniper family had grown bigger by several new recruits, bringing the squad to over twenty. Most of the new apprentices – 'learning on the job', as Zaitsev put it – were young women. Each had a moving story to tell.

Pretty dark-eyed Gulya was a budding violinist. She'd just joined a famous orchestra when war broke out. So she had to swap her violin for a gun, leave her baby son in Moscow and volunteer as a nurse. All nurses had to learn to shoot, and Gulya had shot several Germans while bringing wounded back from the front. Her schoolfriend, Natasha, had been a drama student, then a nurse in a rifle regiment. She too had used a rifle while rescuing the wounded.

The snipers were now holed up in a brewery basement on the embankment. Its smell combined the mustiness of crumbling masonry with the fragrant aroma of hops and barley. As Salami put it, 'you could get drunk on three nose-bags of air.' Following his nose, he had discovered a couple of crates of beer with twenty bottles amazingly unbroken.

Salami passed round the bottles, prising off the metal tops with his teeth. Everyone, including the girls, gladly swigged the cool beer, smacking their lips and burping.

The sole abstainer was Zaitsev. 'A hunter must keep a cool head at all times,' he always said.

The beer must have made Tania bold, for she found herself chatting away to Zaitsev as if they were the best of pals.

'I can't wait to get at them,' she told him. 'I'll snap them in two, like sticks.'

'Why the sudden steely streak?' he asked, with a faint smile.

'I hate them all. They killed my little brother, and my friend Boris before he had a chance to fire a shot.'

'Well, hatred isn't a bad thing,' he said quietly, 'as long as it doesn't breed impatience.'

She stared him straight in the eyes and said sternly, 'Just tell me what to do, and I'll show you!'

'OK, maybe it's time to put you to the test. We'll be splitting into three groups for the operation.'

She took the beer bottle from her lips and gave him her full attention.

'I'll be leading six marksmen into the building from the front. The new lad, Vadim, will take in another six from the back. Right?'

'Right,' she said more soberly, wondering what this was leading to.

'I want you to monitor enemy traffic from the top floor of the building opposite. OK?'

'Is it occupied?'

'Oh yes. There's a three-man machine-gun crew on the third floor, at the front. You'll have to take them out.'

'What's the back-up?'

'Tolya's your second-in-command, the rest are trainees, women.'

'OK, Comrade Commander!'

She wondered why he'd chosen her and not Tolya as leader. But this was not the time to ask questions.

'Once you're in control of the building, your objective is to pick off the Germans opposite. But this is a combined operation, so don't fire till I give the signal.'

'What's the signal?'

'Three whistle blasts.'

Tania was pleased with herself. Her heart was beating fast, her lips twisted in a snarl unlike the Tania of old; she was determined to make someone pay. All her earlier squeamishness about putting a bullet through German heads had been smothered by Misha's death. Now she was prepared to kill and kill again... until not a single enemy remained alive.

'Kill a German!' she said under her breath, recalling Tolya's newspaper cutting.

This was her first command, in charge of an assault group – eight women plus Tolya.

'I won't let you down,' she muttered to Zaitsev under her breath.

Once she'd been issued with a spare rifle, she spent several minutes running through the drill: hard into shoulder, right index finger on trigger, line up target, adjust sights, steady... Fire! Allow for distance, wind speed and background... In her head she could already hear the bullet smacking into a German. Who knows? Maybe it would be Misha's hangman.

Having gone through the motions, she called her group together and went over the same drill with them.

Suddenly Zaitsev shouted, 'Let's go!'

They all shook hands, some hugged. Tania pulled each of her nine snipers to her in a reassuring embrace, kissing them on both cheeks. When she came to Tolya, she gave him a kiss full on the lips.

Then she swiftly turned away with a curt, 'Let's go!'

FIFTY-ONE

As she led her team out of the old brewery, down Sovetskaya Street towards the Universal Stores, Tania sensed a change in the air. In war, of course, everything changes by the day. But there was something else. She noticed it in the soldiers they passed.

They'd come up from the earth, from under the rubble. They were out walking in the afternoon sunshine – soldiers, stretcher-bearers, a postman with his leather bag, two kitchen fatigues with thermos flasks, shoulders back, chests out – and yet there were German dug-outs less than sixty metres away. In just three months, Soviet soldiers had earned the right to walk tall in daylight.

Tania smiled to herself. The Germans had been so cocksure that they'd cut through the city like a knife through butter. In August and September they'd taken one street after another, made themselves at home, danced to mouth organs and accordions. Now, mouth organ and accordion were silent and they were desperately trying to cling on to their positions, hiding underground and behind half-ruined walls.

And it was the snipers' task to drive them out.

Tania's team peeled off from the other two groups. Breaking cover, she led them along the base of the building, holding her rifle in one hand and running, lying flat, then running a few more paces, keeping close to the wall, out of sight.

At what was once a dark red metal door, the ten of them clambered over shattered masonry and twisted metal, making for what remained of the staircase. There were just enough concrete steps left on the stairs to climb, single file, from one landing to the next. As the unit approached its target, shells suddenly whistled in the air and thudded into the building opposite. Through gaps in the wall they could see the entire first floor engulfed in smoke and dust.

This was the signal for the other two sniper groups to rush the front and rear entrances, so diverting the attention of enemy gun crews. Tania's team could hear the *rat-tat-tat* of machine-gun fire above their heads.

'Follow me!' she hissed.

Bursting through the door of the apartment on the third floor, she immediately fired blindly towards the window. One of the machine-gunners threw back his arms as if making a backward dive into a swimming pool, and his body fell from the third floor window on to the rubble below. If the bullet didn't kill him, the fall certainly did.

A second soldier span round, lost his balance and almost fell through the window. A bullet from Tolya helped him on his way. The third man put his hands up in the air: too late. Two bullets hit him simultaneously in the head and the heart.

All three down. First mission accomplished, with no

casualties. Tania was exhilarated, as if she'd just climbed Everest, swum the ocean or beaten the Germans single-handed. That'll show Zaitsev! I can do it! I can break those sticks in two! To herself, she said: that's for Misha, you bastards!

The whole building was now ghostly quiet. She led the unit up the stairs to the top. Just as the coloured markers had shown, the top front apartment overlooked the German-held building opposite. There they were, as cocky as ever, clearly visible through the shattered windows. She rubbed her hands as her unit settled down behind piles of bricks and wrecked beds and chairs. Your time has come, you swine, she thought: your last moments on Earth!

Tania's squad tracked each enemy soldier through telescopic sights, zeroing in on heads and chests. But no one fired. Zaitsev had ordered them to hold back until all the assault groups were in place. Only when he gave three blasts on his whistle, could they pick off their victims in a co-ordinated attack.

But the unexpected happened. Just when they had them where they wanted, two German tanks came rumbling down the street, crashing their way between the two buildings. Behind them, running from doorway to doorway, were two companies of riflemen.

The tanks rammed a Russian anti-tank crew, knocking the gun to one side, and grinding the two bodies beneath its tracks.

Tania held her breath as she noticed Zaitsev dashing

towards the anti-tank gun. He was coolness itself. Calmly, he set it straight, and then did something unexpected: he attached his rifle's telescopic sights to the gun. Peering down the barrel, he adjusted the range-finder and fired at the leading tank. To their astonishment, the shell slotted right through the narrow loophole of the tank, which exploded and burst into flames. What a shot! She'd never seen anything like it. There was no escape for the tankmen inside.

Meanwhile, a long-distance shell from across the Volga knocked out the second tank, sending it careering into the first, and it, too, burst into flames. Just in time, two Germans squeezed out of the turret and joined the few dozen infantrymen crowding the street below.

Tania watched the battle scene unfolding with increasing impatience. Angry at missing the chance of snapping so many 'sticks', she was sitting at the window, fretting over Zaitsev's delay. By the time he returned to his team, it might be too late. She had to take a snap decision: she couldn't let the Germans get away.

'FIRE!' she yelled.

The room exploded in rifle fire: shot after shot after shot – into the thick of the soldiers on the street below and at gun-posts on the second and third floors opposite. When the smoke cleared, she counted seventeen Germans spread-eagled on the churned-up snow. In the building opposite the guns had fallen silent.

'Brilliant. Well done, the lot of you!'

She clapped Tolya on the back and went from one girl

to the next, hugging each of them and grinning all over her face. Her first command – total success!

But she was celebrating too soon.

FIFTY-TWO

Within minutes all hell broke loose, as shells and mortars rained down.

'Take cover!' Tania yelled amid the din. Whether anyone heard or not she would never know. Not that it mattered: there was no cover. The walls were blown in and the roof came crashing down under the furious bombardment. It was a miracle anyone survived, yet Tania escaped with barely a scratch.

She soon wished she hadn't.

As she peered through the swirling dust, she gasped in horror. Bodies were pinned beneath fallen débris, some like tomatoes squashed to a pulp, others with a hand or leg poking from beneath a thick concrete slab.

As Tania staggered round the room, feeling pulses on wrists and necks, closing staring eyes, the terrible truth dawned on her. By opening fire without orders she'd given away the snipers' position to enemy artillery. As a result, she'd been responsible for the deaths of almost all her young charges.

But there was no time for tears. Gulya's voice was shrieking from somewhere. She could hear Tolya's drawn-out groans.

But where were they?

The only visible survivors, besides herself, were

Natasha and another trainee, Senta. Now she yelled at the top of her voice: 'FIND THEM!'

The three survivors rushed about the room, lifting stone pillars, wooden joists, settees, armchairs.

Suddenly, a cry came from Senta: 'Here!'

It was Tolya. The lower part of his body from the chest down was trapped under fallen masonry. There was no blood, but his body had an odd shape, as if he'd been run over by a steamroller.

'Tolya,' she murmured, trying to fight back the tears. 'Hold on, hold on!'

His lips formed a noiseless 'Tania...' before he passed out

Underneath him were a woman's arm and legs – Gulya. She was conscious and able to speak.

'Get him off. I can't breathe.'

There was little they could do except scrape away the smaller débris. Luckily, stretcher-bearers arrived soon after and together they managed to shift the wreckage. But by the time the two badly-injured snipers were on stretchers, it was too late. It brought the number of dead – Tania's dead – to seven.

Tania slowly descended the stairs to report to Lieutenant Zaitsev. He was waiting on the pavement below, his face pale and expressionless. He heard her out in silence. Then, propping his rifle against a wall, he slowly walked up and hit her hard across the face.

'I gave you an order: no firing until my signal! Now look...' His voice broke and he screamed,

'You've killed my *zaichata!* You did it. Your own comrades... You went against the sniper's first commandment: patience. How could you?'

Abruptly, with tears of rage in his eyes, he turned on his heel and marched off, head bowed. She'd never seen him lose his temper before.

Her cheek was smarting from the blow. Her head rang with remorse. Her heart ached for her dead comrades.

She buried her head in her hands and wept.

FIFTY-THREE

For days after the tragedy, Tania cried tears of grief and shame. Nothing could bring them back. They were gone: dead, or gravely wounded – like Tolya, who had lost both legs. All because of her: her stupidity, her impatience. The close band of sisters and brothers had lost seven members at one go. Only fifteen remained.

More snipers would be recruited. But they would have to be trained and battle-hardened. However handy a person was with a gun in the forests of Siberia, the marshes of Belorussia, the mountains of Kirgizia, there was no substitute for the blood and thunder of Stalingrad. It was one thing stalking a wolf or bear, a snow leopard or elk – it was quite another tracking an armed enemy through telescopic sights and, as Tania knew to her cost, waiting hours before firing the single shot that would kill.

No one accused her directly of the deaths. Even so, she felt accusation in each averted gaze, in each hurt glance or sharp tone.

When she visited Tolya in the field hospital, she read the accusation written on his pain-twisted face.

'Tolya, I'm so sorry,' she wept, her head in her hands.

He dredged up a lopsided smile.

'So you should be. If you hadn't taught me to shoot,

I could be taking it easy now in some backwater.'

'You know what I mean,' she said.

'No, I don't.'

As she peered through her fingers, she saw genuine innocence in his brown eyes.

'I gave away our position.'

He closed his eyes and said nothing. After a couple of minutes, he spoke, slowly and hoarsely.

'War... war's about choices. When to attack, when to hold fire. No one can say for certain what's the right moment. Anyway, we may lose a battle, but win the war. That's what counts, isn't it?'

Talking had exhausted him. He lay back, shut his eyes and seemed to fall asleep. Tania stared at the flat sheet below the level of his thighs and sighed deeply.

Slowly she made her way back to the unit.

Despite Tolya's words, she expected to be summoned at any moment. She'd disobeyed orders. She'd caused needless deaths. She'd undermined the whole operation. Soldiers had been shot for less. She was staring execution in the face. At the very least she would be transferred to a Straf battalion – a suicide squad – or receive a severe reprimand that would leave a stain on her character. What she dreaded most was being sent out of Stalingrad, relegated to the rear as an orderly in some godforsaken home for invalids. A bullet in the back of the head was preferable. She was a Stalingradka. She wanted to live and, if need be, die here, fighting to liberate her city.

In the end, she made up her mind. She would ask

for a transfer before they got a chance to kick her out.

* * *

After losing his temper, Zaitsev had treated her no differently from the rest. He was quiet, calm and severe, never smiling, never joking. If he mourned the loss of fallen comrades, he didn't show it; he kept his feelings to himself. Outwardly, he focused on licking the new team into shape.

In the brewery basement, he used the small foreman's office as his operations room. The walls were covered in maps, photos of enemy positions – dug-outs, trenches, fox-holes – and pages torn out of gun manuals. Rifle parts, ammunition, cleaning rags and spare rifles littered the table and floor. A smell of oil and grease filled the air. Against one wall was a bunk that could be raised or lowered.

Her heart in her mouth, Tania forced herself to go and confront him. It was late evening, three days after the tragedy.

At the door she paused, took a deep breath, and knocked. No response. She rapped her knuckles harder on the open door, waiting for him to look away from his maps. He glanced up.

'Excuse me, Vasily Ivanovich, I'd like a word.'

He glanced up with a frown.

'Yes?'

She took that as an invitation and closed the door

behind her. If he was going to fly off the handle again, she didn't want everyone listening in.

'I'd like a transfer.'

He stared at her, uncomprehending, as if she'd asked for a one-way ticket to Siberia.

'What?'

There was no point in beating about the bush.

'I've lost your trust. I can't look my comrades in the eye.'

'Uh-huh.'

'Do I have your permission, then? Or should I wait for the tribunal?'

'What tribunal?'

'For disobeying orders. For... you know... Gulya, Tolya...' Her voice faltered.

Zaitsev was a man of few words. He wasn't comfortable expressing himself in long sentences. Few could fathom his real thoughts. Looking at Tania, he must have seen the turmoil in her mind, the anguish in her eyes.

Clearing his throat, he said hoarsely, 'If you want to go – go. There won't be a tribunal. What for? You didn't kill your comrades. The Germans did. What's done is done. Nothing you can do can bring them back. Right?'

She recognised 'Right' as cover for his awkwardness. But she couldn't answer, 'Right, Vasily Ivanovich'.

He went on, 'You are making a mistake. A big mistake. Only cowards run away. Do you think that's what Gulya and Tolya would have wanted? Do you think that will help us win the war? That's all that counts, isn't it?'

This time she nodded slowly, but said nothing.

'Do you think I've never made a mistake? Of course I have! The vital thing is to learn from your mistake, so you don't repeat it...'

He paused to let his words sink in. When he continued, clearing his throat once more, his voice was soft.

'Listen, Tania, leave if you must. It's your decision. But I don't want you to go. I need you. I trust you. I need you to train new recruits, to set an example. I trust you with my life... I was going to make you my deputy. But now, if you quit...'

His voice trailed off and he waved a hand in the air. He'd run out of words.

'Thank you,' she murmured. Abruptly she took the hand fluttering in the air and pressed it to her lips. 'Thank you.'

He was embarrassed, and pulled his hand away.

'One more thing,' he said huskily. 'I'm sorry I lost my temper. Please forgive me. An unpardonable weakness. Unforgivable... I'm sorry.'

It was his turn to take her hand and kiss it roughly.

***

Tania left the office with a lighter step. The bristles of his chin and chapped lips had contributed to the sweet kiss. The bitter flavour of mahorka tobacco lingered on the back of her hand. Though her heart beat faster, she breathed more easily.

Nothing could make up for her fatal mistake. But his words were balm to her wounds. He was right: to leave the front wouldn't help her dead comrades. Far better to stand and fight. The best contribution she could make would be to become an even better sniper and train others to be as good as her.

In the weeks to come, she spent every minute of her waking hours teaching new recruits how to kill. As a result, the snipers took a terrible toll of the enemy. So deadly was their fire that the Germans were afraid to lift their heads during daylight hours. Officer casualties were alarmingly high: one company lost as many as six commanders in a single month.

Whenever Zaitsev was away, Tania, now promoted to Sergeant, took charge of the unit and led it on missions behind the lines. She was proud of her position – she knew Zaitsev had never entrusted anyone to cover for him or offer a view on tactics. Now he'd often turn to Tania and ask, 'Well, Tania, how do you see the situation?' Or, 'How do you estimate wind speed and distance?'

Looking back, Tania felt grateful to him for talking her round. In terms of winning the war, she knew she was making a contribution: the Germans were on the back foot, demoralised, short of food and ammunition.

The tide was turning.

FIFTY-FOUR

On the thirteenth of November 1942, three waves of Junker 87s flew over the city. They dropped their bombs on artillery batteries along the Volga's eastern bank. Then they flew away, never to return.

The bombing ceased.

It left a totally unnatural calm. After eighty-two days of constant bombing – from dawn to dusk – after eighty-two days of non-stop, deafening thunder and thick, choking smoke, the black dust clouds above Stalingrad lifted and soldiers no longer had to keep a wary eye on the sky.

Now a lone spotter plane would appear, as regular as clockwork, at sun-up and sun-down; and sometimes Messerschmitts would zoom overhead, disappearing over the horizon.

On the ground, however, there was no let-up in the battle. Mortar shells whistled and howled, machine-guns chattered away like magpies, tanks and rifles punched the air and there was no limit to the shells and bullets.

And yet, as the New Year approached, the front grew steadily quieter: just the occasional dull crack of a sniper's rifle, a burst of machine-gun fire, the whistle of a night flare.

Something was about to happen. From trenches and

ruins, bunkers and cellars an excited buzz could be heard on both sides of the river. Rumours ran riot.

The snipers joined in the speculation.

'Has Fritz had enough?' suggested Vadim. 'Has he run out of bombs?'

'Or planes?' said Lena.

'Or pilots?' added Salami.

Zaitsev was as wary as ever.

'It could be a trick.'

A clue came at the end of January, when the commander, Colonel Batyuk, summoned Zaitsev and Tania to a briefing.

'Intelligence reports,' he said, 'have pinpointed the German command bunker within the city.'

'Where?' asked Zaitsev.

'Closer than you'd think,' said the Colonel. 'In the Universal Stores!'

'The Univermag!' exclaimed Zaitsev in disbelief. 'That's only half a kilometre away.'

'That's right,' confirmed the Colonel. 'Close enough for snipers to flush the enemy out.'

Colonel Batyuk looked hard at Tania.

'Sergeant Belova, I'm assigning you to this mission.'

Zaitsev went red in the face.

'Comrade Colonel, may I respectfully remind you that I am in charge of the sniper unit. If the mission is so important, I'll do it myself.'

'No! Sergeant Belova will take charge. In any case...' he hesitated, '...the order comes from the highest level.'

He looked meaningfully at Zaitsev.

'Look, Vasily Ivanovich, this mission is not only of the utmost importance to Army Command.' He hesitated again, before saying quietly, 'It's too risky for you to be involved. Understood?'

Even Zaitsev couldn't argue with Army Command.

Turning to Tania, Colonel Batyuk dropped his bombshell.

'This is top secret. Your mission is to capture von Paulus, Commander of the German Sixth Army.'

Tania took a deep breath. What a responsibility! To capture the man who'd led the attack on her city. How she'd love to put a bullet through his heart! Of course... she might not return alive. Even if she got past the guards and reached the German commander, what then? How would she escape? It was surely a suicide mission – which is why Zaitsev had been spared. Still, she was prepared to die for her city and her country, as Misha had.

FIFTY-FIVE

They set off in the early evening, as darkness was drawing in. The four of them, all women, moved in single file, keeping to the shadows and following a route marked out through the streets. Tania went second, just behind Lena, her second-in-command, to pass instructions to the front and rear.

Lena was a crack shot, but sometimes she was clumsy, which worried Tania.

'Lena, for God's sake,' Tania hissed, 'tread carefully.'

It made no difference. Lena continued to stumble along, tripping over stones in the dark.

Then she stumbled once too often. As they were passing a row of half-demolished shops, she stepped on a mine.

The explosion was a jumble of blinding flash and hurricane blast that sent them all sprawling in the roadway. For a minute no one stirred. No noise. No movement. Just stunned silence.

Lena caught the full blast of the explosion. It lifted her into the air, flung her down and ripped open her stomach.

As she lay bleeding and unconscious in the gutter, someone rushed forward. It was Zaitsev. He had disobeyed orders, following the four girls at a distance.

Now he feared the worst.

By a miracle, two of the girls were only slightly hurt, mostly cuts and bruises; Tania felt a sharp pain in her stomach where shrapnel had caught her.

'Are you OK?' Zaitsev asked.

'I'm fine,' Tania said, gritting her teeth.

Once Zaitsev and Tania had checked on the two conscious girls, they turned their attention to Lena.

Tania looked down on her best friend with pity and horror. The girl was lying in the road, bleeding badly. One arm was bent back at an unnatural angle, the other was no more than a bleeding, fingerless stump. One of her army boots had been blown off by the blast.

As Tania bent down to move it, she gasped – Lena's foot was still in it!

'She's losing a lot of blood,' Zaitsev muttered. 'Needs medical help urgently.'

'Just as well you were passing,' said Tania ironically. 'You can get a stretcher crew. We've a job to do.'

Zaitsev saw that he had no option. He disappeared into the shadows.

Suddenly Lena's eyes flickered open and she spoke in a low voice.

'Tania, don't leave me.'

What was Tania to say? The remaining three had to get on, but how could they leave Lena to die alone?

'No, we won't leave you,' Tania promised. 'As soon as they get you to hospital, they'll patch you up and you'll be as right as rain.'

Lena gave a faint smile. Tania prayed that Zaitsev would bring help soon, before the numbness wore off and Lena felt the full pain of her wounds. Meanwhile, she must take Lena's mind off her injuries.

'Have you ever been kissed, Lenochka?'

Lena was silent for a while.

'Once, by Vova.'

'What was it like?'

'Wet. Sticky. You?'

'Only by Mama and Papa, if you don't count a kiss on the hand.'

'Was it nice?'

'All right. A bit rough, like a spiky hair-brush. Who's Vova?'

Lena suddenly let out a shriek as the pain shook her.

'Come on, come on,' called Tania under her breath to Zaitsev.

Lena screwed her eyes shut and Tania did her best to staunch the flow of blood. While she pressed a torn cloth to Lena's stomach, one of the other girls tied part of her tunic round Lena's leg as a tourniquet.

All at once, Lena's face grew calm. She opened her eyes and spoke quietly, but clearly.

'Vova was a boy... at school.' She sighed. 'When the Germans came, they shot him and his parents.'

'What for?' asked Tania.

'They hid a Jewish family in their attic. A local policeman gave them away...' Her voice trailed away as she slipped into unconsciousness.

Shortly after, Zaitsev arrived with two women stretcher-bearers. Lena's pulse was very weak.

'Bye, Lena, see you after the war,' Tania whispered in her ear. 'Don't worry. We'll make them pay!'

She tore herself away.

FIFTY-SIX

Tania and her two companions hitched their rifles on their backs and hurried on. Tania could feel a dull ache at the pit of her stomach. But she clenched her teeth and pushed on.

It wasn't long before they reached the main square.

'See that big grey building in the distance?' she whispered. 'That's our target, the Univermag.'

All three peered through the gloom at what remained of the once-grand department store. A hazy moon cast light on its bullet-marked granite walls, tall, broken windows and crumbling archways.

'Follow me!' she muttered hoarsely.

They flitted like ghostly shadows from building to building, past the Gorky Theatre, moving stealthily, one step at a time. The most dangerous part was crossing roads where they were in the open. Tania's wound was slowing her down, but she limped along as best she could.

At each halt she would wait patiently for clouds to cloak the moon.

Then, 'Go!'

All three dashed helter-skelter for the safety of another ruin or a burnt-out tank in the middle of the road. Fortunately, there were no searchlights or shells lighting up the city. For the first time in nearly three months, Stalingrad was dark and silent.

Tania knew from the briefing that only the Univermag still held out. And somewhere in that vast building was von Paulus. No doubt he was guarded by men who would go down fighting for their commander-in-chief.

After almost an hour the sniper group reached the offices, linking up with the assault unit that was to act as cover. All they had to do was cross the road, march in and say 'Hands up!' Well, maybe it wasn't quite as easy as that.

This was Tania's big moment: whether she lived or died, she wasn't going to mess it up this time.

A young officer greeted them.

'Lieutenant Fyodor Yelchenko. I was told there were four of you.'

'Sergeant Tatiana Belova,' she said, saluting. 'There was a slight hitch. Now we're three.'

'We go in at midnight.' He looked at his watch. 'After our Katyushas have softened them up.'

No sooner had he spoken than, with a fizz, a wail and a roar, the rocket-launchers opened up on the Univermag.

Whoosh! Whoosh! Whoosh! The rockets flashed overhead, exploding into the bricks and mortar of the store.

Half an hour later, the deluge ended just as suddenly as it had started. This was the signal for Lieutenant Yelchenko to yell, ' Let's go!'

He led the charge, with his men spraying bursts

of flames into the building. Soon the entrance was a mass of flames and crashing débris.

The sniper group kept close on the heels of the soldiers as they dashed through the flames; they expected a hail of bullets, but were surprised. No bullets. No blast. No machine-gun burst. Nothing. Perhaps the Germans had tunnelled their way out? Or were they all dead?

As the three snipers crept through the shattered plate-glass doors, they were met by a strange sight. Beneath a creaking sign saying SAUSAGE stood a German officer waving a white flag.

Lieutenant Yelchenko approached him cautiously, motioning his men back and the snipers to accompany him.

They followed the German down two flights of stone steps into the basement.

Nothing prepared them for what they found down there. The basement was full of hundreds of German soldiers, dirty, blood-stained, stinking, staring, wild-eyed with fear... and hope – surely a group of women would take pity on them?

The German officer spoke Russian, making it clear they wanted to surrender.

Lieutenant Yelchenko was uncertain.

'Where's your Commander-in-Chief?'

At first the German looked puzzled.

'We surrender,' he said, including all the soldiers with a wave of his arm.

Tania took up the questioning.

'You surrender to Lieutenant Yelchenko. But our orders are to take Colonel-General von Paulus prisoner. Where is he?'

The tone of her voice made it clear she meant business.

With a weary nod, the German gestured for the three young women to follow him. He led them down a long corridor, past stores and offices, vaults and wine-cellars, piles of rotting cabbages and mouldy cheese, until they came to a room at the very back of the building. Again, the officer nodded – this time towards the closed door.

Tania waved the man back, signalling to her companions to cover her, rifles at the ready. She had no idea what to expect. A booby trap? An élite guard to fight?

Her head was throbbing, the pain in her stomach was almost unbearable. It was all she could do to stand straight. But she wasn't going to give up now; not with such a valuable prize at stake.

Counting to three under her breath, she drew back her right boot and kicked the door open.

FIFTY-SEVEN

Nothing…

As Tania glanced round the room, rifle raised, she noticed an iron bed on the far side. The gaunt figure of a man was lying there, his head resting on his hands.

At first she thought he must be dead – probably from poison, when all seemed lost.

As Tania approached, the man swung his long legs off the bed and sat up.

He was unshaven, his face ashen and lined, one eye twitching nervously. In a split second she noticed two other things: an Iron Cross at his neck, and highly polished jack-boots. Somehow the smart boots struck her as an odd contrast to the grey-black stubble on his chin. Was this really the chief of the once-invincible Sixth Army?

'Are you Colonel-General Friedrich von Paulus?' she asked, in a croaky voice.

He looked up sharply. For the first time he saw the three girls. Their presence was obviously not to his liking, for he rattled off loud curses in German. Then, blinking his right eye rapidly, he spoke slowly and clearly in Russian.

'No, I am not! I am not Colonel-General. I am Field-Marshal. Yesterday the Führer promoted me.'

Tania tried again.

'Are you Field-Marshal Friedrich von Paulus, Commander-in-Chief of the German Sixth Army?'

'*Jawohl!*'

He stared at her helplessly, as if unable to accept that he was surrendering to a girl.

Tania felt unsure: should she be respectful to this officer or treat him as enemy? It was a bizarre situation: a young girl in a dusty tunic pointing a wobbly rifle at someone who towered over her – and he one of Hitler's trusty generals – or rather, field-marshals.

He glanced down at her blood-soaked trouser leg, perhaps wondering whether to fight his way out. He evidently thought better of it and, with a weary shrug, stepped towards her.

'Follow me, please,' she said politely. To her companions, she added, 'Stassya, take one side; Sveta – bring up the rear. Let's go.'

The tall German commander put on his cap and greatcoat and stepped into line.

The procession moved down the corridor, past the German prisoners, who stared at the curious sight. The Field-Marshal gazed straight ahead.

'Have you searched him?' asked Lieutenant Yelchenko.

'No.' Tania replied.

Yelchenko quickly frisked the officer, finding only a nail file in his pocket along with papers confirming his new rank.

Von Paulus looked at him with contempt.

'Do you really think that I, a German officer, would slit my throat with a nail file?'

Lieutenant Yelchenko rang headquarters for orders. A car was to be sent immediately.

Tania smiled grimly. They'd done it!

It wasn't long before a black limousine drew up outside the Univermag and von Paulus was rushed away to army headquarters.

There was no chance of the snipers hitching a lift. They'd done their job; now, in all the excitement, they were forgotten. Tania and her two companions were left to make their own way back to the sniper base.

Only when Tania emerged into the cool night air did she feel the full force of her wound. The numbness had worn off and the throbbing pain increased with every step. She couldn't go on. After a dozen paces, she fell to the ground.

***

It wasn't until she was on the other side of the Volga that she came to. By one of those freak coincidences of war she was in the same ambulance that had taken Lena on her final journey. Though Tania wasn't surprised to hear that Lena had died, the news hurt her more than her own injuries.

FIFTY-EIGHT

Several months passed. After operations to remove pieces of shrapnel from her legs and stomach, Tania was evacuated to a sanatorium far from the battlefield. Her war was over.

While she was lying in her hospital bed, she had a visitor: a stocky man in a black leather jacket.

'Dad!'

'Hello, my little pigeon! How are you?'

'Fine. What are you doing here?'

'That's a nice way to greet your poor old father! I'm here to see you before I leave for Berlin. Yes, we're going to chase those wolves all the way back to their lair.'

Tania smiled happily. Her stomach wound was gradually healing, though it would be a while before she could walk.

Her father had spoken to the doctor and he had some news to deliver.

'You'll live, Tanechka. You'll soon be as right as rain. Doctor says so.'

He stroked his chin and stared at his feet.

'There's just one thing... You won't be making me a grandfather. That's it, straight.'

He looked up to see how she was taking it. Tania put on a brave smile.

'You're too young to be a grandfather,' she said. 'Anyway, Dad, I need a husband first.'

He quickly changed the subject.

'I've traced your mum and Vanya. They're safe and sound in the Urals. Once this wretched war's over, we'll all be together again.'

'All except Misha,' murmured Tania. 'Our little cobbler.'

Dad turned his face away. He knew about his son's death.

'Well, Tanechka, mustn't tire you out. I have to get back to my regiment by noon tomorrow. I'll bring you a new dress from Berlin, OK?'

He bent over and kissed her on both cheeks, then turned quickly so that she didn't notice his tears, and he was gone.

FIFTY-NINE

Stalingrad was coming back to life. News of the German surrender slowly filtered through to the survivors. At first, no one believed it.

But as the truth finally sank in, dazed human beings began to emerge from the city's underworld, stumbling crazily about, kissing and hugging everyone they meet, crying happily on each other's shoulder.

'Is it over? Really?'

'Are you sure?'

Out of the rubble came several thousand more people, blinking into the dazzling light of sun and snow, dirty and ragged, their bellies swollen with hunger, their eyes full of the horrors they'd seen.

They were the lucky ones. The Battle of Stalingrad claimed over a million dead – far more than any battle in history.

But the city had stood firm and its victory marked a turning-point: the beginning of the end of the war. Stalingrad would go down in history for the fighting spirit of its people who didn't know when they were beaten.

***

As for Tania, she screwed tight her eyes and the events

of those six months flashed before her. What she'd been through. What she'd seen that no sixteen-year-old should ever see. How she'd done things no young person should ever do.

In her mind's eye, she saw the scorching heat of August when the sky filled with deadly mosquitoes. She remembered digging Nina out of the sandy soil; people staring at the crashed plane; smoke and flames from Mamayev Kurgan; her gun battery; pools of beetroot soup on the floor of her home.

She saw the choking dust and moonlit nights of September as she bounced along in old Timofei's Studebaker; eating American corned beef; holding a rifle for the first time; taking the road back to Stalingrad; the grey-haired mother holding out her arms; those silent columns marching into the mouth of hell.

She saw the drenching rains of October when Sergeant Vlasov saved the barge from sinking; the swampy smell of the Volga; the sun shining through the factory's one remaining chimney; the anguish of killing her first German; tears trickling through Tolya's fingers.

She saw the biting winds and swirling snowflakes of November when she had come face to face with German prisoners; those trinkets and human hair; the icy river and the stinking sewer; German kitchens, Aunt Moosya and her orphans; Misha's ice-cold feet; Boris's letter; Zaitsev's rage at the deaths of his zaichata; Tolya's terrible wounds.

She saw the bitter frosts of December and January; the scratchy record playing its song to Milady Death;

Lena stepping on a mine; the capture of von Paulus.

All this she saw.
Six seconds.
Six months.
Six lifetimes.

NOTE ON THE STORY

This story is based on actual events and people who took part in the Battle of Stalingrad, from the German invasion in early August 1942 to Field-Marshall Paulus' surrender on 31st January 1943. The crushing Soviet victory changed the course of the Second World War. Hitler had planned to capture the strategic port on the Volga River and sweep behind the Soviet lines to Moscow. It was therefore crucial to make a stand at Stalingrad. Thanks to the heroism of the Soviet soldiers and people, the German army met its first defeat of the War.

Tania Belova's story closely follows the true story of Tania Chernova. All the characters are based on real people. After the war Tania married, but could not have children owing to her war wounds. Awarded the Red Star for bravery, she died in her native city in 2002, at the age of 80.

Tolya Chekhov, who accounted for the deaths of 256 enemy soldiers, returned to his native Kazan as a welder after being invalided out of the army. Decorated with the Red Banner and Red Star, he died aged 44.

Lieutenant Zaitsev eventually reached Berlin with the victorious Red Army. After the War, he managed an engineering works in the Ukrainian capital of Kiev. Many times decorated for killing over 300 enemy soldiers, he was made a Hero of the Soviet Union. He died in 1990 at the age of 76.

Many of the events portrayed in this story are described in war despatches from Stalingrad by the writer Vasily Grossman. Thus, Tolya Chekhov features in 'An Everyday Stalingrad Story' on 20 November 1942, the Trophy Room in 'The Stalingrad Offensive' on 1 December 1942, and the Red October Factory battle in 'Today in Stalingrad' on 1 January 1943, all in the army newspaper Red Star.

I would like to express my gratitude to Vasily Grossman's daughter, Yekaterina Vasilievna in Moscow, and to all Stalingrad veterans and staff at the Battle of Stalingrad Museum, especially Svetlana Argastseva, for their kind assistance during my visits to their city over the past forty years.

Svetlana it was who, in the summer of 2002, introduced me to an elderly woman sitting modestly in one corner of the Museum. It turned out to be Tania Chernova – the real sniper of Stalingrad – who told me her unforgettable story.

James Riordan has written ten novels for young people. His first book, *Sweet Clarinet*, won the NASEN award in 1999 and was nominated for the Whitbread Prize in 1998. *Match of Death* won the South Lanarkshire Book Award in 2004 and *The Gift* was nominated for the NASEN award in 2006. His first novel for Frances Lincoln was *Rebel Cargo*.

He first visited Stalingrad in 1959, making subsequent visits in 1963 and, most recently, in 2006, when he met Tania Chernova. Having studied Russian in Birmingham and Moscow, he lived, worked and travelled extensively in Russia for five years, and has presented several BBC radio programmes on Russia. He is Emeritus Professor of Russian at the University of Surrey, and has chronicled his time in Russia as a Communist footballer in *Comrade Jim: The Spy Who Played for Spartak*.

Rebel Cargo

James Riordan

Abena is an Ashanti girl sold into slavery and
transported on the notorious sea-route from
West Africa to Jamaica's sugar plantations. Mungo
is an English orphan who becomes a cabin boy,
only to be kidnapped and sold on as a white slave.
Mungo risks life and limb to save Abena from death,
and together they plan their escape to the
Blue Mountains, to a stronghold of runaways ruled
by the legendary leader Nanny. But can Mungo
and Abena get there before the Redcoats and
their baying bloodhounds drag them back…?

Based on events and records of the time, the
novel unflinchingly describes conditions of slavery
in the early 18th century – a time when profits
took precedence over humanity – and ends
on a note of hope.

Yellow Star

Jennifer Roy

In 1939, the Germans invaded the town of
Lodz, Poland, and moved the Jewish population
into a small part of the city called a ghetto. As the
war progressed, 270,000 people were forced to
settle in the ghetto under impossible conditions.
At the end of the war, there were 800 survivors.
Of those who survived, only twelve were children.
This is the story of Sylvia Perlmutter,
one of the twelve.

Lines in the Sand
New Writing on War and Peace

Edited by Mary Hoffman and Rhiannon Lassiter

Talented writers and illustrators from all over
the world have come together to produce this book.
They were inspired by their feelings about the conflict
in Iraq, though the wars covered in this collection
range from a 13th-century Crusade through the
earlier wars of the 20th century to recent conflicts
in Nigeria, the Falklands, Kosovo and South Africa,
right up to what was happening in Iraq in 2003.

With over one hundred and fifty poems,
stories and pictures about war and peace,
Lines in the Sand offers hope for the future.

All profits and royalties to UNICEF

Give Me Shelter

Edited by Tony Bradman

Sabine is escaping a civil war...
Danny doesn't want to be soldier...
What has happened to Samir's family?

Here is a collection of stories about children from
all over the world who must leave their homes
and families behind to seek a new life in a strange land.
Many are escaping war or persecution. All must
become asylum seekers in the free lands of the West.
If they do not escape, they will not survive.

These stories, some written by asylum-seekers
and people who work closely with them,
tell the story of our humanity and the fight for
the most basic of our rights – to live. It is a testimony
to all the people in need of shelter and those
from safer countries who act with sympathy
and understanding.

Angel Boy

Bernard Ashley

When Leonard Boameh sneaks away from home
to do some sightseeing, little does he know that
his day out is about to turn sinister. Outside
Elmina Castle, the old fort and slave prison,
groups of street kids are pestering the tourists,
and before Leonard knows it, he is trapped
in a living nightmare.

Set in Ghana, this chilling chase adventure is
one you'll never forget.

From Somalia, with Love

Na'ima B. Robert

Safia knows that there will be changes ahead but
nothing has prepared her for the reality of dealing
with Abo's cultural expectations, her favourite brother
Ahmed's wild ways, and the temptation of her cousin
Firdous' party-girl lifestyle. Safia must come to terms
with who she is – as a Muslim, as a teenager,
as a poet, as a friend, but most of all, as a daughter
to a father she has never known. Safia must find
her own place in the world, so both father and
daughter can start to build the relationship
they long for.

From Somalia, with Love is one girl's quest to
discover who she is – a story rooted in Somali
and Muslim life that will strike a chord
with young people everywhere.

Black and White

Rob Childs
Illustrated by John Williams

Josh is soccer-mad and can't wait to show off
his ball skills to his new classmates. After all,
he is the nephew of Ossie Williams –
the best footballer in the country.

Josh's arrival helps to give shy Matthew more
confidence, but it is not welcomed by Rajesh,
the school goalkeeper and captain. With important
seven-a-side tournaments coming up, will the
players be able to settle their differences
and work together as a team?

Mixing It

Rosemary Hayes

Fatimah is a devout Muslim. Steve is a regular
guy who's never given much thought to faith.
Both happen to be in the same street the day
a terrorist bomb explodes. Steve is badly injured
and when the emergency services arrive, Fatimah
has bandaged his shattered leg and is cradling his
head in her lap, willing him to stay alive. But the
Press is there too, and their picture makes the
front page of every newspaper. 'Love across the divide,'
scream the headlines. Then the anonymous 'phone calls
start. Can Steve and Fatimah rise above the hatred
and learn to understand each other? But while
they are breaking down barriers, the terrorists
have another target in mind...

THE
SNIPER

Nominated for the CILIP Carnegie Medal 2010

"An exciting, well-researched story."

The Irish Examiner

"Every moment of the chilling account should change
the perspective of readers. An important story."

Carousel

"From the first page this is a powerful and heart-rending story.
Well known for his sensitive and perceptive writing about
adolescence in extreme situations, Riordan has produced
an extraordinary and thought-provoking book.
This is a story that lingers in the reader's mind
and should certainly be an award winner."

School Librarian